For Brenda Ogden,
My BRILLIANTLY rambunctious English teacher.
This is all your fault!
SB

For my effervescent Aunty Jill and Uncle Keith X
SL

First published in Great Britain in 2018 by Simon & Schuster UK Ltd
A CBS COMPANY

3 5 7 9 10 8 6 4
Simon & Schuster UK Ltd
1st Floor, 222 Gray's Inn Road
London
WC1X 8HB
www.simonandschuster.co.uk
www.simonandschuster.com.au
www.simonandschuster.co.in
Simon & Schuster Australia, Sydney
Simon & Schuster India, New Delhi

A CIP catalogue record for this book is available from the British Library.

PB ISBN 978-1-4711-6383-8
eBook ISBN 978-1-4711-6384-5

Printed and bound by CPI Group (UK) Ltd, Croydon, CR0 4YY
Simon & Schuster UK Ltd are committed to sourcing paper that is made from wood grown in sustainable forest and supports the Forest Stewardship Council, the leading international forest certification organisation. Our books displaying the FSC logo are printed on FSC certified paper.

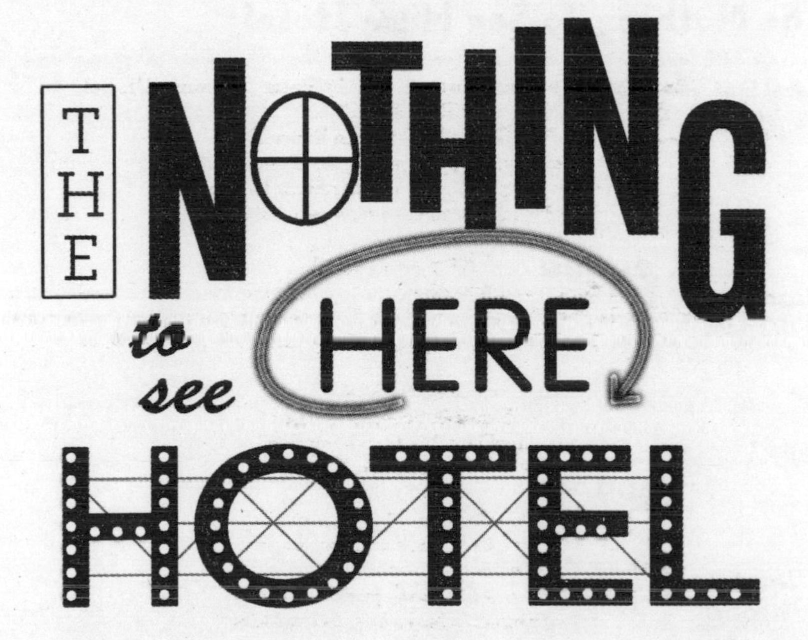

STEVEN BUTLER

ILLUSTRATED BY STEVEN LENTON

SIMON & SCHUSTER

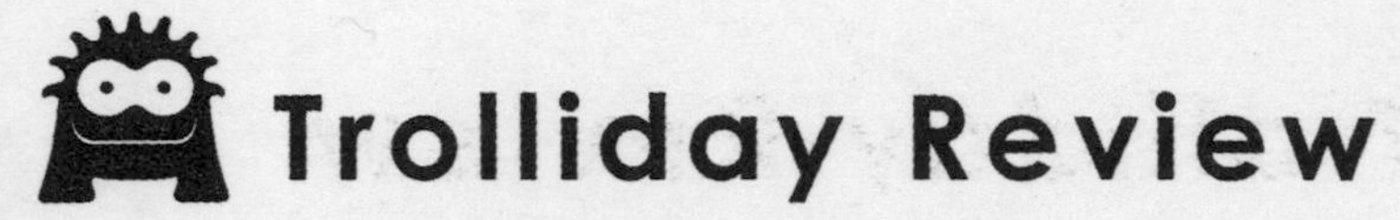

You are viewing user reviews for The Nothing To See Here Hotel, Brighton

The Nothing To See Here Hotel

NB. Everyone is welcome at The Nothing to See Here Hotel (except humans... NEVER HUMANS!)

1,079 Reviews #1 of 150 Hotels in Brighton

Brighton Seafront UK BN1 1NTSH 00 11 2 334 4556 E-mail hotel

Francesca Simon

Reviewed 2 days ago

'A rip-roaring, swashbuckling, amazerous magical adventure. Comedy gold.'

Jeremy Strong

Reviewed 13 days ago

'A splundishly swashbungling tale of trolls, goblins and other bonejangling creatures. Put on your wellies and plunge into the strangest hotel you will ever encounter. This is a hotel I hope I never find! Wonderfully, disgustingly funny.'

Cressida Cowell

Reviewed 29 days ago

'Hilariously funny and inventive, and I love the extraordinary creatures and the one thirty-sixth troll protagonist...'

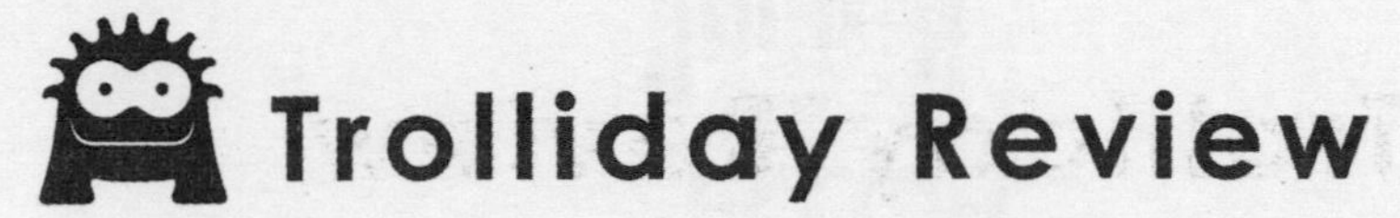

You are viewing user reviews for The Nothing To See Here Hotel, Brighton

The Nothing To See Here Hotel

NB. Everyone is welcome at The Nothing to See Here Hotel (except humans... NEVER HUMANS!)

1,079 Reviews #1 of 150 Hotels In Brighton

Brighton Seafront UK BN1 1NTSH 00 11 2 334 4556 E-mail hotel

Reviewed 33 days ago

Liz Pichon

'This hotel gets five slimey stars from me...'

Reviewed 54 days ago

Jacqueline Wilson

'A magical hotel, known for its exclusive unique clientele. The chef is to be congratulated for inventing Bizarre Cuisine. All staff very friendly, but avoid the Manager (especially if you're wearing a cat-suit).'

Reviewed 75 days ago

Kaye Umansky

'What a fun hotel! Book me in immediately!'

WELCOME TO
THE
NOTHING
to see
HERE
HOTEL

WELCOME TO
THE NOTHING
to see HERE
HOTEL

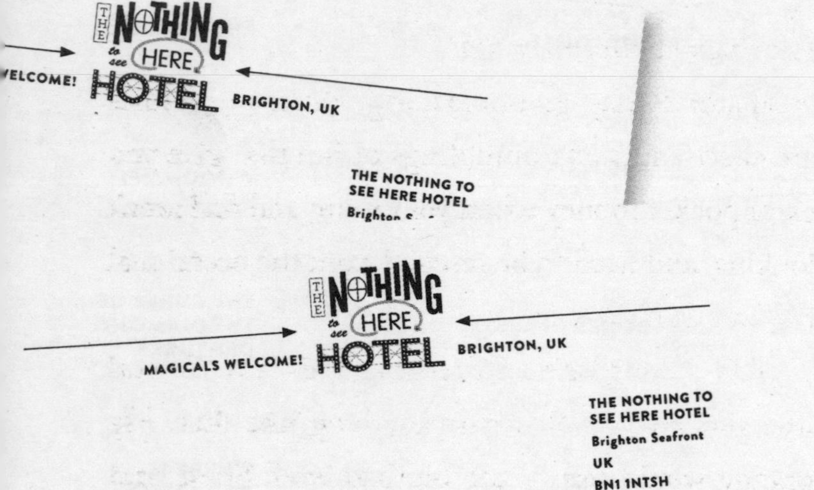

Are you in need of a relaxing getaway or somewhere to escape the daily grind of lair lurking, bridge bothering or humdrum haunts? **The Nothing to See Here Hotel** is the place for you. We take honkhumptious pride in being the best secret holiday destination for magical creatures in the whole of England.

Whether it's soaking your scales in our pool, sampling the toothsome delicacies created by our spider-cook extraordinaire, Nancy (her porcupaties smothered in sticky giblet jam are to die for), reading up on a curse or two in the library, or just cooling your bunions at our luxurious mud spa, we guarantee there's something for everyone.

To confirm your booking, please fill in the attached form.

NOT ALL OLD LADIES ARE NICE

Let's talk about *grandmas* ...

In storybooks, grandmas or grannies or nannies are *sweet* and *short* dumplings of fun that give you extra pocket money when your mum and dad aren't looking, and need to be rescued from the occasional big bad wolf.

BUT ... this isn't a storybook. This is really-real life, and *my grandma* isn't anything like that. My granny would terrify the big bad wolf. She'd beat him to a pulp. She'd gulp him down, chewing and slobbering as she did so, and belch out his bones before breakfast.

Oh ... I should probably tell you ...

My granny is a **TROLL**.

A mean one.

THE NOTHING TO SEE HERE HOTEL

Phew! Now I've told you the truth about my granny, the rest of what I'm about to tell you won't sound quite so bonkers.

My name is Frankie, by the way ... Frankie Banister. Hello!

I know you're probably already thinking that I've had my brains scrambled or I'm loop-de-loop crazy – a troll for a granny?! But we've only just started: keep reading and I'll explain everything, I swear. You'll begin to believe me in no time ... my granny really is a hulking, stinky great troll, and not a single word of what I'm about to tell you is a lie.

Go on, just a few more pages ...

Ready?

Here we go ...

MY GRANNY THE TROLL

About a hundred years ago, back in the olden days when people wore tall hats and everything was in black and white, my great-great-great-grandad, Abraham Banister, went for his usual morning walk along the beach and *KAPOW!* he changed the history of our family FOREVER.

Right out at the far end of the seafront, near the rocks, my gramps spotted something strange. Something **VERY** strange and **VERY** large.

According to my dad, Grandad Abraham was a collector of rare plants and animals. He used to travel the world, searching for weird and exotic things … so what he spotted on that black-and-white morning must have made his curly moustache twistier than EVER.

Abe spotted a troll girl (a trollette) doing her laundry in the open mouth of a huge sewer pipe and having a good old sing-song to herself.

You guessed it: that troll girl was my great-great-great-granny, Regurgita Glump, and before anyone could scream, 'NO! WAIT, ABE! SHE'S HIDEOUS!' the two of them fell madly in love, ran off and got married in a proper slobberchopsy troll ceremony down in the sewers under Brighton high street.

DON'T PANIC! The rest of the story isn't all gross and lovey-docious, I promise.

Fast-forward a hundred years and here I am: Frankie Banister, the newest member of the bunch.

You can imagine our family tree is a crazy one. It's dotted with trolls and humans and harpies, with the occasional witch and puddle-nymph thrown into the mix. My uncle Stodger is a bogrunt!

My dad, Bargeous, is what's known as a halfling, and my mum, Rani, is completely human, so that makes me a quarterling, I suppose. I know that I'm one thirty-sixth troll.

You probably wouldn't notice I wasn't fully human at first glance. My hair is always messy and it hides my pointy ears most of the time, so the only thing that really gives it away is the colour of my eyes. Just like Dad and all my other relatives going back up the family tree to Granny Regurgita, mine are copper-coloured, like shiny pennies. It's the first sign of having troll blood.

Anyway, I really want to tell you all about where I live.

One hundred years after my great-great-great-grandparents built it, my family still live and work in **The Nothing To See Here Hotel**. It's the best secret holiday destination for magical creatures in the whole of England. You weren't expecting that, were you?

Poor old Grandad Abraham popped his clogs years and years before I was even born, but Granny Regurgita is still about. Trolls live *hundreds* of years longer than people.

My granny calls herself the manager of the hotel, but she hardly ever leaves her bed, so me, Mum and Dad do all the hard work. Every day we run around like human bumper cars, trying to keep a bunch of magical creatures from wrecking the place. Weird is normal to the Banister family.

Are you starting to believe me? Ha! I thought you *might* ...

I could spend hours and hours telling you about the hotel and describing what it looks like, but you'd probably get super bored and throw this book across your bedroom, screaming, 'I HATE FRANKIE BANISTER!' so here's a map instead. Maps are WAY more fun and you'll find out loads more later in the story.

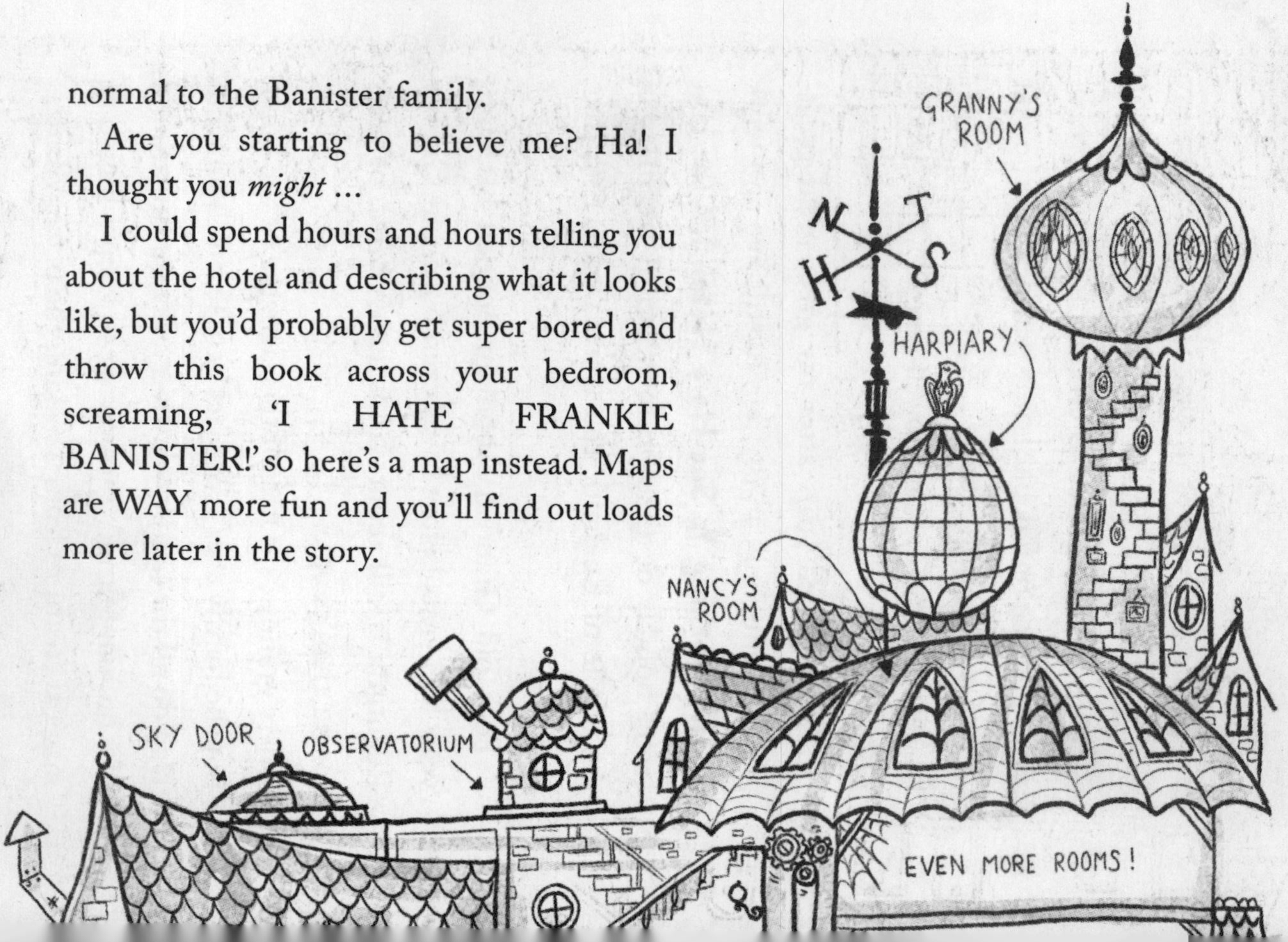

HOTEL
MORE ROOMS
ROOMS
RECEPTION
SEA DOOR
MY ROOM!
LIBRARY
LIFT SHAFT
SWELKY TANKS
MUD SPA
KITCHEN
CONSERVATORY

I know what you're thinking ...

How can the hotel be that much of a secret if it's so **MASSIVE**? Anyone with half a brain would spot something strange going on in seconds if they walked past. But that's where a little bit of **troll magic** comes in ... You see, the front of the hotel looks just like any other you might find by the seaside and that's the only part that human eyes can see, so no one suspects a thing! The rest of the hotel is enchanted by Granny Regurgita and is completely invisible.

The only time there's ever a clue that a huge, magical hotel is standing in plain sight at the end of Brighton seafront is when a seagull flies into one of the invisible towers. It's pretty funny. If someone was looking hard enough, they might spot a seagull come swooping over the town, heading for the sea, and **WALLOP!** The poor bird stops in mid-air, then squawks off in a whirl of feathers, looking more confused than a T-rex in a tutu.

But no one ever notices. All the people that come and go along the seafront are way too busy buying ice creams and splashing about to pay any attention to surprised seagulls. That's how the hotel has managed to stay secret ever since Abe and Regurgita opened it all those years ago.

We also use a couple of crafty tricks to stop any human tourists from wandering in by mistake. First of all, the visible part of the hotel is always kept shabby and old-looking. The windows NEVER get washed and the outside hasn't had a lick of paint since the place was first built.

Then there's a spell on the front steps that fills the noses of any non-magical person who stands on them with their most hated smell in the world. It's brilliant! Let's imagine that the smell of dog poo is the worst thing you can imagine. If you put even one little toe on our front steps, your nostrils would instantly be full of the strongest stink of it. Ha! Humans soon think twice before ringing our doorbell.

As if that wasn't enough, Mum and Dad's final trick is to pretend to be angry guests of the hotel. They call the local newspapers once a week and rant about how horrible and dirty the rooms are, or how disgusting the food is, and put rubbish reviews up online.

Dad is so proud of all our 'ZERO STAR' reviews that he frames them – they're all hanging above the reception desk.

"DISGUSTING!"
"The worst hotel EVER!"
"THERE WAS A FLY IN MY SOUP!"

So . . . here we are on page eighteen. You've read this far so by now you must believe me. You're probably thinking that to be a human kid living in an invisible hotel with magical creatures must be

BRILLIANT, and I suppose I can see why. Things can be downright crazy around here, which is fun, but it's not ALL fairy wishes and sparkly crowns and stuff.

Don't get me wrong. I love my weird home and being part troll is pretty great, but it's easy to forget all of that when you've been helping Mum clean up after Mr Vernon, the Stink Demon, has been to stay for the weekend ...

Anyway, I'm getting sidetracked. The REALLY exciting stuff started on the night of the HUGE storm.

I was climbing the three hundred and ninety-nine steps to Granny Regurgita's tower bedroom, and things at the hotel were about to get interesting ...

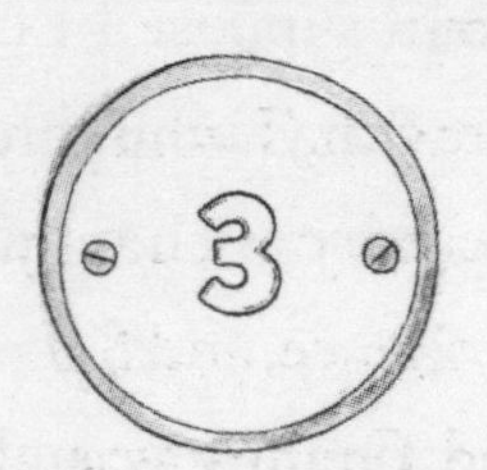

GRANNY REGURGITA

Visiting Granny always gives me a gloopy, nervous feeling in the bottom of my belly. Granny Regurgita is just plain terrifying; even Dad gets twitchy whenever she hobbles down from her tower once in a blue moon to see what's going on in the hotel.

When Granny's in a bad mood (and she always is), she can make a blood-crazed tiger look like a cute little kitten.

Three hundred and ninety-seven ...

Three hundred and ninety-eight ...

I finally got to the top and stopped to catch my breath. Outside, rain was lashing against the windows, and this high up in the tower everything creaked and groaned. I was half expecting the whole thing to topple over in the wind so I didn't want to hang about.

'Just get it over with,' I whispered to myself, then gulped and knocked on Granny's bedroom door. There was a long silence, and for a minute I thought I was in luck and Granny was already asleep. Fat chance!

'Come in, boy,' she finally croaked from the other side.

I nudged the door open with my foot and her familiar stink of mould and rotten vegetables wafted out onto the landing. It's sour enough to sting your eyes and make you sick, I swear. No matter how many times I brought Granny Regurgita her food and bedtime mug of pondweed tea, I'd never get used to the disgusting pong of that wrinkly old husk.

Inside Granny's bedroom, everything was inky dark. I stood in the light of the landing and squinted my eyes, trying to spot her in the gloom.

'Hurry up, you useless carbuncle!'

I could hear the sound of her slug lips smacking together.

'Granny's hungry . . . What have you brought me?'

Just then, lightning flashed outside and I caught sight of her copper-penny eyes glinting in the darkness.

'**GET ON WITH IT, YOU LITTLE SNOT!**'

I took a step inside her bedroom and shuffled towards the spot I'd seen her eyes flash seconds before.

One of the perks of being the great-great-great-grandson of a troll is that I can usually see in the dark, just like it's daytime – it's one of the cool things about being a human kid with troll blood in your veins – but this was magical darkness filling the room . . . thicker, colder and blacker than the normal kind. Granny Regurgita loves to wrap herself in it like a blanket. Even when it's daytime and her windows are wide open, Granny's room is like the inside of a deep cave.

'I can't see, Granny,' I said. 'Can you put the lights on?'

'No!' she barked. 'I like it dooksome and

dungeonly.'

'Please, Gran—'

'**NOOOO!**' A bent spoon from last night's dinner sailed out of the gloom and bounced off the top of my head with a painful TUNK.

'Ow!' I yelled.

'OH, stop your griping,' Granny hissed, 'and **GIVE ME MY GRUB!**'

'I'm going to drop it!' I knew that would work. Magical creatures are SO greedy and the thought of missing out on food or drink terrifies them.

Granny Regurgita grunted in the dark. She snapped her crusty fingers, and hundreds of candles in jam-jar lanterns suddenly lit themselves. The room twinkled into view and there she was, my enormous, grizzly grandma, hunched in her bed like some slobbering, hairless buffalo.

She was a monster to look at. A grey-green hulk in a filthy nightdress, with fat scarlet toadstools sprouting across her shoulders and head. Her eyes glinted copper as another bolt of lightning flashed outside.

'Hello, Granny,' I said, trying not to look too scared. (Don't forget, she's the size of a bear and grumpier than a yeti with a headache.)

'FOOD!' she yelled, reaching for the plate in my hand. 'NOW!!'

I took another step closer and Granny's pet thistlewump, Gurp, uncurled at the end of the bed and growled at me. I hate thistlewumps, and

I especially hate Gurp. It's a football-sized ball of thistles and thorns, with twiggy feet sticking out at the bottom and very sharp teeth. I'd lost count of how many times the horrible little shrub had bitten me. Now, it just blinked its yellow eyes at me, then scampered across the blanket and snuggled under Granny's arm.

'Gurp, my twigling,' Granny said, chuckling and cooing.

Before Gurp had come along, Mum and Dad tried out a few pet cats to keep Granny company, but they kept disappearing. For ages we thought she'd scared them off and they'd made a quick getaway across the rooftops of the hotel, until she belched up a huge ginger furball one morning. How were we supposed to know that Granny had a taste for tabbies on toast? That's why Mum and Dad settled on a thistlewump. It's the only thing too prickly to chew.

'Here you are, Granny,' I said. I held out the plate of cockroach quiche and she snatched it wildly from my hands. I barely had time to blink before she threw back her head and emptied the whole thing down her gullet, plate and all.

'**DRINK!**' she barked as soon as she was done chewing.

I handed her the pondweed tea and she did the same thing, pouring it straight into her huge mouth, followed by the mug.

'Delunktious!' she sighed.

Once she'd finished licking her lips and picking

her teeth, she lowered her eyes back towards me and stared. For a minute I wasn't sure if she was going to say anything, so I waited. You never know ... maybe today would be the day she'd actually say thank you.

'Don't just stand there oogling, you little pimple,' she finally said. '**Bog off!**'

I didn't need telling twice. I spun round and ran for it.

But ... I told you that things got really interesting when I was visiting my Granny Regurgita in her tower bedroom and, as you must surely know by now, I don't tell lies.

Just as I reached the door, Granny gasped.

A FLASH IN THE DARK

'**Boy!**' Granny practically spat the word at the back of my head.

I turned and saw her sitting bolt upright, copper eyes wide, and ears twitching backwards and forwards like she was straining to hear something. She snatched her rusty ear trumpet from beside the bed and jammed it into one of her ears.

'What's wrong?' I asked, watching her face crease up with concentration.

'Shhhhh!' she hissed. 'I thought I just heard—' She gasped again, then hurled herself out of bed, dropped the ear trumpet on the floor and clomped to the window. Granny could move pretty fast when she wanted to, but it was normally only when she was scrambling for leftovers.

'What?' I ran and joined her at the window. With the jam-jar lanterns all burning brightly, it was hard to see anything except our own mismatched reflections staring back at us. 'What did you hear?'

Granny ignored me. She clicked her crusty fingers for a second time and every candle in the room instantly extinguished itself. Suddenly the outside world rushed into view far below. There, in the light of the street lamps, were the other hotels and restaurants that lined the seafront. Peering out of the window, I could see the waves thundering up the beach, and every flash of lightning cracked the sky in two, lighting up the raindrops like stars.

'What did you hear?' I asked again, but she was still ignoring me. Her eyes were fixed on the night sky above the ocean.

'There!' she suddenly yelled and pointed into the storm.

I squinted and tried to see what she'd spotted.

'There, boy! **LOOK!**'

Another flash of lightning lit up the sky and I

finally saw what Granny was pointing at. High above the sea was a huge black raven frantically beating its wings against the wind and rain. It whirled upwards, then vanished back into the night.

Another bolt of lightning flashed and I saw the raven was closer this time and ... and ... there was something riding on its back. A small figure, hunched forward and holding on for its life.

'What is it, Granny?' I asked. 'A fairy? A pook?'

'A goblin,' Granny said. 'It's a messenger.'

All the hairs on the back of my neck tingled with excitement. Who was sending us a message by Goblin Post?

'**QUICK, BOY!**' Granny barked at me. 'It won't last long out there. Run and let it in!'

QUICK!!!

I leaped down the tower steps, two then three at a time.

Down and round the corner,

down and round the corner,

down and round the corner …

'Come on, Frankie,' I huffed to myself as I sprinted.

My brain started racing. The storm outside was getting worse: it looked like something from my *Real-Life Adventures of Captain Plank* books. What if the goblin messenger gave up and flew away?

I wasn't about to miss out on the chance of some real excitement. Only BRILLIANT things arrived by Goblin Post.

I reached the door at the bottom of the tower

steps and barged through it without checking if anything—

'*UUUGH!*' Before I could stop myself, I ran straight into Nancy, the hotel cook. She screamed with fright and toppled backwards onto the carpet, waggling her legs in the air. All eight of them.

This is probably a good time to tell you that Nancy is a giant spider – and I mean a *really* giant one! An Orkney Brittle-Back to be precise. She's the last of her kind, and has been working at the hotel ever since it opened.

If Nancy stands on her back legs, her head touches the ceiling, and she can easily reach all the way across the kitchen to grab the salt and pepper when she's cooking at the stove. So she's a whirlwind when it comes to making food for lots of guests.

Don't think big scary spider from a monster movie though. There's nothing monstrous about Nancy. It's also pretty hard to find her scary when she speaks with a Scottish accent, and wears spectacles, a flowery apron, fluffy slippers on her four back legs and has a blueish/purplish perm.

'Oh, Frankie!' she said, blinking all eight of her eyes at me. 'Where are you off to in such a hurry?'

'No time to explain,' I puffed. All I could think about was getting to Mum in reception, and letting the raven and its goblin rider into the hotel. I was still so far away. There were about a squillion hallways and staircases between me and the ground floor. 'Storm! Raven! Goblin!'

Nancy clambered back to her feet, then touched my forehead as if checking for a temperature.

'Are you all right, my lamb?'

'A goblin messenger, Nancy! Out in the storm!' I finally managed to shout. 'I have to tell Mum.'

Nancy's face lit up. 'OOOOOH! Goblin Post? That's unexpected.'

'QUICK!'

Nancy nodded and a look of determination spread across her facc. She grabbed me under the arms and swung me over her shoulder.

'Right you are, ducky.'

With that, Nancy raced along the top-floor hallway with me clutching tightly to her bristles. I loved riding on Nancy's back. There aren't many things that can outsprint an Orkney Brittle-Back.

She click-clacked down the corridors like an eight-legged rocket, sometimes running right up the wall and across the ceiling to avoid guests that were coming and going from their bedrooms to see what all the noise was about.

'**Excuse us!**' Nancy shouted as we ran past Madam McCreedie, an ancient banshee who had checked in yesterday. The poor old thing screamed in shock so loudly that all the lights bulbs down the corridor exploded.

In no time at all, we had reached the top of the great spiral staircase that wound its way straight down through the middle of the hotel to the reception hall on the ground floor.

'Here we go, Frankie,' Nancy huffed over her shoulder. I squinted my eyes and gritted my teeth as she started leaping down the stairs, ten steps at a time. '**WE'LL BE THERE IN A JIFFY!**'

As we rounded the next bend of the great staircase, I spotted Lady Leonora Grey wafting her way up the steps towards us. Usually she haunts

'**DO YOU MIND?!**' Lady Leonora screeched as she vanished behind us. 'How rude!'

We were nearly halfway down the great staircase now, but I'd already spotted more guests in the way as we rounded the next curve. A family of impolumps were hobbling their way upstairs, dragging their suitcases behind them. They looked up with wide eyes as we galumphed closer and closer.

'Oh, bother,' Nancy said as we sped downwards. I could almost hear a plan forming inside her head. 'Hold on, Frankie, and, whatever you do, don't let go.'

Before I even had time to think about wetting my pants with fear, Nancy looped a silky strand of web over the banister and, just before we ran **SMACK** into the petrified impolumps, she **JUMPED!**

Hampton Court Palace, but every summer she takes a break from scaring tourists and comes to haunt the hotel instead.

Ghosts are so weird! They don't need rooms or beds or toilets; instead they rent stairs to wander up and down, moaning to themselves. Not much of a holiday, if you ask me!

'Woe is me!' Lady Leonora was shrieking to herself. 'DESPAIR!'

'Watch out!' I shouted.

'**GET OUT OF THE WAY!**' Nancy joined in, but it was obvious Lady Leonora wasn't listening. Ghosts NEVER listen. They're too busy wailing and gnashing their teeth to pay attention to other people – even a boy riding a giant, speeding spider!

'Fine!' Nancy grunted and, without bothering to slow down, she ran straight through Lady Leonora. I love running through ghosts. Mum and Dad always tell me off if they catch me doing it, but it's SO much fun. It feels like ice-cold popping candy all over your skin.

THE SKY DOOR

When I told Nancy to be quick, I never imagined I'd be screaming like a rabid rooster, and clutching her perm, as we fell head first towards reception below.

It's all a bit of a blur after she jumped. We plummeted like a twelve-limbed comet through the centre of the spiral staircase and that's about all I can remember ... oh ... except for the loud **TWANG-ANG-ANG** as the strand of web finally caught and we stopped just above the floor. I opened one eye and almost burst out crying at the sight of the black and white tiles, only centimetres away from my face.

'Oh, lovely,' Nancy said, beaming to herself as if absolutely nothing had happened. She put me down, then snipped the web with a sharp swish of her arm and stood up, smoothing out her apron. 'I haven't made a good string in ages. Might use that to knit some gloves ...'

For a second the terrifying leap made me completely forget what I was doing, or why we were trying to get downstairs so quickly. Then I saw Mum standing with Ooof, the hotel's ogre handyman (a handyogre, I suppose) on the other side of the big, circular entrance hall.

'Hello, Frankie,' Ooof called, waving his

enormous green arms and accidentally smashing a vase of flowers that stood on the end of the reception desk.

Mum was gawping at me from behind the desk. Her eyes were the size of teacups and she looked like she'd just swallowed a wasps' nest.

'Mum!' I scrambled to my feet and tried not be sick or fall back down. My head felt like someone had reached inside and swizzled it up with an egg beater.

'**FRANCIS!** What on earth is going on?' Mum barked. I hate it when people call me Francis. Mum and Dad only use that name when I'm in trouble. It's their secret weapon. 'Well, I'm waiting?'

I ran round the fountain in the middle of reception, and up to the stone desk where she was drumming her fingers angrily. Ooof copied her, thudding his fingers down, but grinning instead of scowling.

'Are you **CRAZY?**' Mum said. Her face had turned from shocked to furious. 'I can't believe you and Nancy were **BUNGEE JUMPING! IN**

FRONT OF THE GUESTS!'

'Mum, we weren't. Listen ...'

'You're in serious trouble, Francis!'

For a second I half expected to see steam coming out of Mum's ears.

'Do you know how dangerous that is? **DO YOU? AND WHAT DO YOU HAVE TO SAY FOR YOURSELF, NANCY?'**

If Granny Regurgita hadn't been on Dad's side of the family, I would have sworn I could see a bit of her in Mum just then.

'Ummm ... Mrs Banister ... Rani ... I can explain...' Nancy looked ashamed and fiddled with the frilly edge of her apron.

'Mum, you've got to listen to me!'

Mum opened her mouth to speak again, but I knew if I let her throw a wobbly she'd be yelling for hours and I wouldn't be able to get a single word out.

'**INCOMING!**' I screamed in her face as loudly as I could. My voice echoed round the reception hall and back up the staircase. It was like a thousand Frankies all yelling, one after another, and it certainly did the trick.

Mum stuttered with surprise and her forehead wrinkled up. She closed her mouth, opened it and closed it again.

'*What?*' she finally said after a few seconds.

'There's a messenger outside.' My heart felt like it was about to play a tune on the inside of my ribcage. '**A GOBLIN MESSENGER ... OPEN THE DOORS!**'

'A messenger?' Mum said, jolting to attention. 'Why didn't you say so?' Mum was very proud of the hotel's customer service and would never leave a magical creature outside in such terrible weather.

'Ooof, find Mr Banister,' said Nancy. 'He'll want to know about this.'

'Ooof find,' said the ogre, and clomped off towards the kitchens.

The reception desk was carved out of stone and had twisty, trollish writing engraved around the edges. It was part of the troll magic that kept the hotel invisible, and in the centre of its flat surface were three large keyholes circled by gold symbols of a fish, a snake and a bumblebee.

'Sea door or sky door?' Mum said, pulling out a large brass key that she wore on a chain around her neck.

'**SKY DOOR!**' I shouted. I was far too excited to speak normally.

With that, Mum pushed the key into the keyhole with the bumblebee symbol and turned it with a loud CLUNK.

Suddenly the whole of reception sprang into life under our feet. The spirals of black and white floor tiles that circled outwards from the fountain started to rotate in different directions, whirring like the gears of a clock.

'*Wheeee!*' Nancy chuckled, doing loops of the room in the opposite direction to me. 'I feel like I've had a few too many sips of bluebottle brandy.'

I had to choke back a big laugh as a sofa rattled past with Gladys Potts, the werepoodle, flailing about on it. She'd been in human form, chewing an old newspaper, but now she started howling with surprise as her ears turned into curly white puffballs and a pompom tail burst through the back of her dress. She quickly changed into full poodle mode and scampered out of the reception hall, in the direction of the conservatory.

The snake lock opens the front door, and if Mum had turned the key with the fish symbol, the fountain in the middle of the room would have slid away to reveal a deep well that leads all the way under the hotel and out to sea. That door was mostly used by mermaids and sea-swelkies on their holidays.

The mechanism in the floor began to slow and reception stopped spinning. I looked up and saw the last corner of the ceiling slide away, ten floors up. Now there was nothing between us on the ground and the storm high above, and rain started to fall straight down through the centre of the great spiral staircase.

'Can you see anything?' Mum yelled over the rain.

Nancy put an arm round me and we both stared upwards, squinting. I gripped my toes and hoped the goblin messenger had noticed the sky door clanking open. But through the hole, where the ceiling had been, I could only see night and rain, until—

BOOOOOOM!! Thunder and lightning crashed together. The storm was right overhead. The blackness flashed white and I saw the shape of the raven and its rider hurtling down towards us.

'**SKRAWK!**' The bird flew through the sky door like a bullet. Its wings were folded flat against its sides, and for a second I panicked that it might be out of control. The bird was flying, beak downwards, straight towards the floor. If the goblin rider didn't pull out of this nosedive soon, they'd both be smashed to bits against the tiles.

'Oh no!' Mum gasped under her breath.

'**SKRAWK!**' the raven replied as it continued to hurtle down through the centre of the staircase. Suddenly I could understand why Mum had been so angry when me and Nancy had jumped from the staircase. This was terrifying to watch.

Nancy screamed and turned away as I clamped my eyes shut and prepared to hear the horrible crunch of raven and goblin bones slamming into the floor.

I waited ...

And waited ...

Nothing.

I opened one eye and looked up.

There, perched on the outstretched arm of the water-witch statue in the middle of the fountain, was the biggest raven I'd ever seen. It scraped its talons against the statue's hand and flapped its wings, showering raindrops in all directions. '**SKRAWK!**'

The raven was wearing a tiny pair of leather

goggles and had a bridle and reins around its beak. On its back there was an ornate saddle with dozens of pouches, jars and cloth satchels attached, and in the saddle sat a bedraggled, soaking-wet goblin.

He pulled his own pair of goggles off and patted the raven on the head.

'Another perfectorus landin', if I do say so meself,' he said in a voice that sounded like old paper being torn.

'H-hello,' I said.

The goblin grinned a wonky grin at me and winked.

''Ello ...'

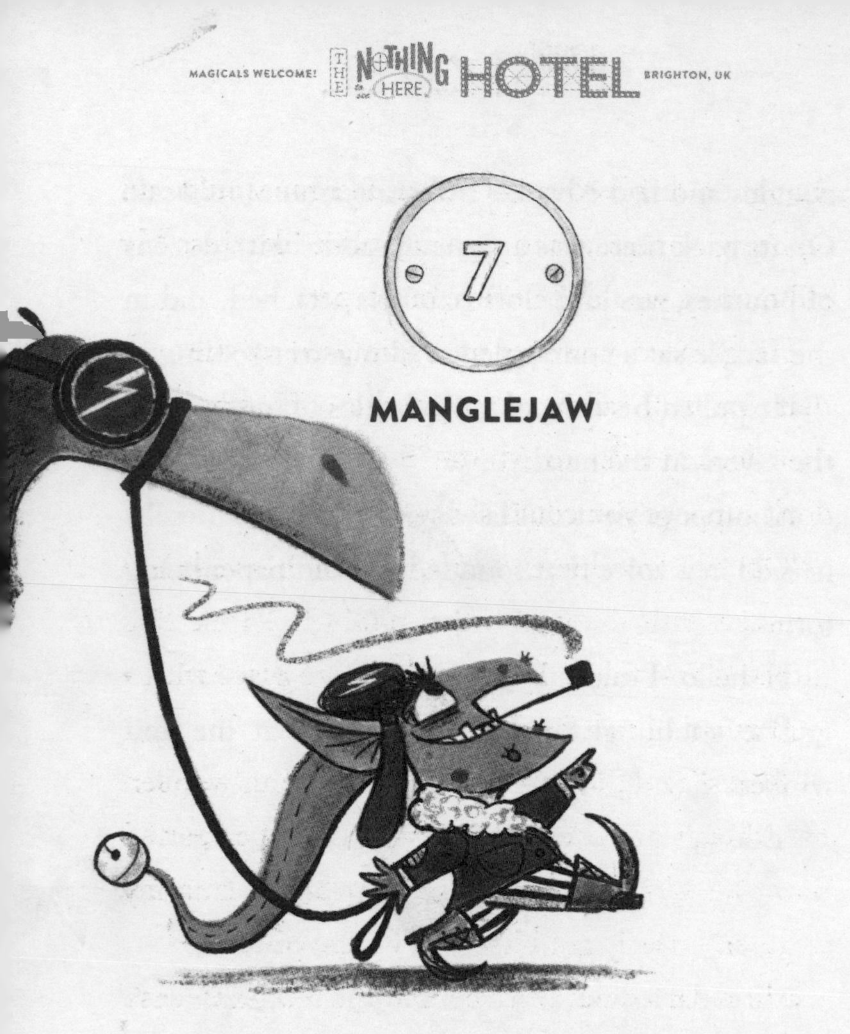

7

MANGLEJAW

'So this is The Nothin' To See 'Ere 'Otel?' the goblin said, looking around reception and nodding to himself. He had a thin clay pipe wedged between his teeth, and a wisp of yellow smoke wafted up and floated above him like a wreath. It was as if the rain and the wind hadn't touched it at all. 'Who'd have thought a scabberous old skrunt like me would end up bringin' messages to a poshly place like this? My old mumsy wouldn't believe 'er peepers.'

He glanced upwards and grimaced at the rain that was still falling through the open sky door, then looked over to Mum. ''Scuse me, lady ... I don't suppose you could shut that, could ya?'

'Oh my goodness! Sorry,' Mum blurted and fumbled with the key in the bumblebee lock. She turned it and the ceiling slid back into place with a loud groan of metal cogs. 'There we are.'

'Fanks!' said the goblin. He pulled off his woollen hat and squeezed the rainwater out of it, then patted down his blood-red uniform. 'Terrible tantrummy weather. I nearly got blown to Timbukthree!'

Mum darted out from behind the reception desk and joined me and Nancy beside the fountain.

'Now, can we get you a cup of tea, Mister ... ?'

'I ain't no "MISTER"!' the goblin laughed. 'Manglejaw's me name ... Muggerty Manglejaw ... but just plain old Manglejaw will do for now.'

'Hello, Manglejaw,' Mum said, pulling her best

'Welcome to the Hotel' smile.

'What a lot of hellowin',' Manglejaw said. 'I ain't got time for tea though, I'm afraid. A postal goblin's work is never done, and I've got grabfuls of letters to deliver yet, and—'

'What's going on?' Everyone jumped and spun round as Dad wandered into the reception hall from the library with a stack of books in his hands. He'd been in there all afternoon, trying to sort out an Ink Blott problem. A family of Blotts had checked into the pages of the books and rearranged all the letters to make more room for their ink luggage.

'Did I hear the sky door?' he said.

'Dad, it's a goblin messenger!'

Dad looked at me, then at Mum and Nancy. He peered over his glasses and frowned, scanning the room for goblins.

Nancy coughed politely and pointed up to where Manglejaw and his raven were perched on the statue.

''Ello,' Manglejaw said. He gave a little nod of his head.

'Oh, gosh!' said Dad, nearly dropping the pile of books.

'Postal Goblin Manglejaw at your service,' said Manglejaw.

'Welcome! Can we get you a cup of tea?' Dad nodded back.

'Manglejaw doesn't have time,' said Mum.

'S'right,' said Manglejaw. He yanked on the raven's reins and flew to the floor. 'None o' that for me, fankin' you. I'm 'ere to do a job.'

The little goblin hopped off his raven's back, walked around to a large pouch hanging off the side of the saddle and started rummaging inside. It had been ages since I'd seen a goblin up close, and I couldn't stop staring.

Living in a hotel for magical creatures, I see all sorts of weird and bonkers things every day, but this was unusual even for us. Goblins mostly hated being near humans and always kept themselves to themselves, so we hardly ever had them stay at the hotel.

I'd forgotten how short they are too. Now that

Manglejaw was standing on the floor, he was only about as tall as my knee, and his wrinkly pale skin made him look more like an oversized turnip than a living, breathing creature.

''Ere we are,' Manglejaw chuckled, pulling out a tiny scroll of gold paper.

A tiny scroll? I had been hoping for a chest of magical treasure, or a dragon's egg, or at the very least a cool spellbook from some long-lost relative. We did have a couple of witches in the family after all …

'Righty,' said Manglejaw. He unrolled the scroll and read in a loud voice.

A ROYAL DECLARATION
FROM THE PALACE OF THE
BARROW GOBLINS!

Mum gasped and steadied herself on my shoulder.

'The Barrow Goblins? What do they want with us?'

'They never come up from underground,' said

Dad. 'Do they?'

All the hairs on the back of my neck prickled. There are loads of different species of goblin in the world and I'd NEVER seen a Barrow Goblin. They lived miles underground near the centre of the earth.

Prince Grogbah, son of Queen Latrina, and heir to the throne of the Dark and Dooky Deep, is tired on his tinkly toes and will be coming for a holiday from his Royal Duties at The Nothing To See Here Hotel. Make feasts, funlies and festivibles in preparation for his divine arrivalling or else you'll all be dead. Thank you!

Nobody spoke.

Mum gawped at Dad, and Dad just shook his head in amazement.

'A prince?' Nancy finally said.

'A g ... goblin prince,' Mum stammered. 'Coming here?'

'We'll need to redecorate the entire hotel,' said Dad. He started running on the spot in panic. 'We'll need to get ten times more food, and fill up the cellars with frog grog, and landscape the garden, and extend the swimming pool, and replace ALL THE FURNITURE!'

'When is he coming?' Mum asked Manglejaw, her eyes practically popping out of her head.

'Errrm ...' Manglejaw mumbled. He frowned at the scroll and reread the message. 'Ummm ...' Then he turned it over and read something on the back of the paper. 'Ah, 'ere it is ...'

Everyone held their breath.

'Tomorrow,' Manglejaw said with a grin. 'At noon.'

8

YOU'VE MADE IT THIS FAR!

Right ... let's stop here for a teeny second and talk about all the stuff you've read so far.

I bet you never imagined these kinds of things were going to happen? I also bet that, by now, you would have expected to say, 'Yep! I was right ... that Frankie Banister is just a complete nutter.'

Admit it ... HAHA!

WELL, YOU DIDN'T!

Here we are at Chapter Eight and I know you can't wait to read what happens next ... and since the next few hours were mostly full of everyone running around like headless chickens, trying to get everything ready for the prince, I say we skip all the boring cleaning bits and jump to the next morning when Grogbah was due to arrive.

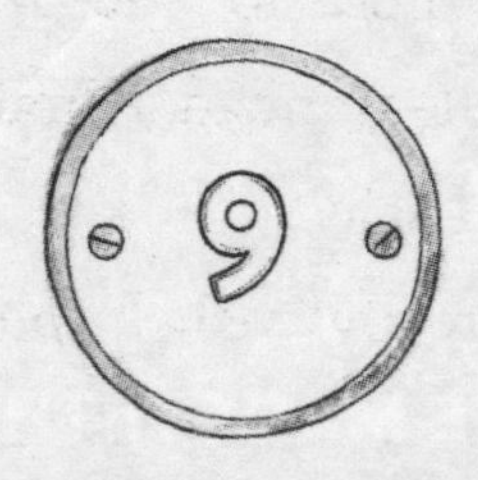

THE NEXT MORNING

'Francis!'

I opened one eye ...

'Francis! Wake up and get down here!' It was Dad's voice, coming from the dented, trumpet-shaped contraption that poked out of the wall just above my bed. It's an annoying gadget that trolls invented hundreds of years ago called a yell-a-phone.

Down in the kitchen was the main speaker, which was attached to a machine that looked a bit like an old-fashioned typewriter, but each button connected it to a different room of the hotel. I could picture Dad down there now, clicking the button for my bedroom and howling away up the pipes.

I sat up, rubbed the sleep from my eyes and

gave my usual nod to the framed picture of Great-great-great-grandad Abraham on the wall. 'Morning, Abe,' I said.

I sometimes really wish I could have met him just once.

In the picture, Grandad Abraham is trekking through deep jungle and there's a boy of about my age with green eyes and jet-black hair standing next to him. I don't know who the kid is, but I wish it could have been me instead. I would have loved to have gone on adventures with good old Abe.

I yawned and looked around my bedroom. It was just how I liked it.

I can never find anything when things are tidy. But, if my room is perfectly messy, I know exactly where everything is. My *Ministry of Mutants* comics go on the floor, my clothes are in a mound at the end of the bed, and Grandad Abraham's collection of *The Real-life Adventures of Captain Plank* books are piled up on the windowsill.

Captain Calamitus Plank is a big celebrity in the magical world. He's an ancient goblin pirate and, if what Granny says is true, he was a good friend of Abe's back in the old days. I love reading about his swash-bungling quests. They're my favourite. I even have a poster of him above my fireplace.

Oh, speaking of fireplaces ...

I glanced over at it.

'Morning,' I said.

Nothing moved.

Don't worry. I don't spend my mornings talking to fireplaces. I'll explain ...

I reached out my hand and wriggled my fingers.

'Wakey-wakey.'

Slowly the glowing coals at the bottom of the grate shifted and opened one eye.

'Morning, matey,' I said. 'Who wants a TREAT?'

The pile of coals uncurled and Hoggit, my pet pygmy soot-dragon, leaped onto the bed.

Haha! I've been waiting for just the right moment to tell you about Hoggit. He might only be the size of a little dog, but Hoggit's the COOLEST pet in the world ... well ... he is at the moment. One day, when he finally breathes fire, he'll be the HOTTEST pet in the world! Dad says I need to be patient and Hoggit will become a proper little inferno one day.

'Hello, boy,' I said as Hoggit flopped over my lap and started purring.

'***Grrrroooooor***,' he moaned, looking up at me with wide eyes. He huffed a tiny smoke ring into the air, which was his way of saying ***FEED ME!***

Suddenly I felt guilty. I'd only used the T.R.E.A.T. trick to get him out of his fireplace bed, and now I didn't have anything to give him.

'FRANCIS, NOW!' This time it was Mum's voice coming out of the yell-a-phone. **'YOU'VE SLEPT IN! THE PRINCE IS DUE ANY MINUTE!'**

'Come on, we'd better go, boy, before they put Granny on the yell-a-phone!'

Hoggit wagged his tail at me, then jumped off the bed and onto the big squishy armchair.

I quickly threw on some clothes from the laundry pile, and glanced at myself in the mirror. My trousers were wrinkly and my T-shirt had a stain on it, but what did that matter? Everyone would be far too excited to care about boring stuff like that.

I walked over to the armchair and sat down, pulling Hoggit onto my lap. Then I clicked the little dial in the arm of the chair to just the right combination and braced myself as it juddered and started lowering down through the floor.

You see, my bedroom is in a secret spot above the library with no doors or stairs leading up to it. That's why I think it's the BEST room in the whole hotel. Great-great-great-grandad Abraham used it as a private place to keep all his books and specimens and notes about strange animals, so they didn't get muddled in with the others in the library below, and designed a special chairlift that only he knew the code for.

After lots of begging, Mum and Dad finally let

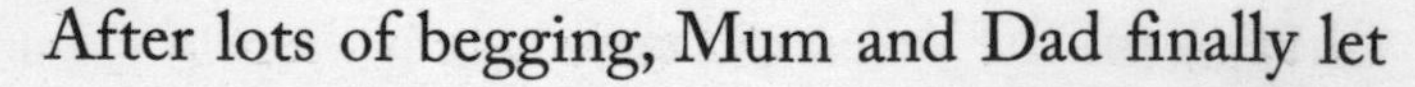

me move into the room as a present on my birthday a few years ago. They gave me the dial codes for Abe's armchair and, once I'd learned them by heart, I fed the piece of paper to Hoggit, so only I know how to make the chairlift work and Mum can't keep barging in and telling me to tidy up.

We were rattling past the Magical Dark Romance section when I looked down and saw a gaggle of dust pooks skittering across the floor in a line. '*Quickly, quickly, quickly,*' they were singing to themselves. The dust pook at the end of the line peered up and saw me and Hoggit riding the chair down the track in the wall by the bookshelves. '*Quickly, quickly, quickly,*' it yelled at me in its squeaky little voice. '*Quickly, quickly, quickly.*'

The chair reached the library floor with a bump, and, with Hoggit trotting along beside me, I ran after the potato-sized pooks to find everyone.

It was exciting to know I was going to see a Barrow Goblin today, but I didn't know why Mum and Dad were in such a flap. Goblins were gross, dirty creatures. What did they care if there was dust on the mantelpiece or wrinkles in the bed sheets?

I turned through the archway that led from the library into reception. For a second I thought it was completely deserted, until I spotted Mr Croakum, the gardener, halfway up the stairs, decking the banister with garlands of flowers.

'Frankie, there you are!' he said, smiling down at me. 'You'd better hurry out to the garden. Everyone's there, and your mum and dad are in a bit of a panic.'

Horacio Croakum hadn't been working for us very long. He'd arrived at the hotel as a human health inspector, then never left when he discovered it was actually stuffed full of magical creatures. You see, Mr Croakum is a froggle, although you'd never know it. He's what's known as a 'blender' in that he looks just like a human, but when he opens his mouth a ten-foot-long tongue shoots out and can grab something on the other side of his potting shed. He'd spent his entire life hiding his MASSIVE secret, not realising there was a whole magical world out there! And then he found us. Now he's married to Mrs Venus, a GIANT fly-trap plant that

Grandad Abe brought to the hotel as a tiny sapling, back when he was exploring in the Peruvian jungle all those years ago.

Mrs V is pretty cool to look at with her red and green teeth, and tendril arms, but we have had a few problems recently because she keeps falling asleep with her mouth open on the lawn. Just last month, Hoggit ran in there after his ball and nearly got gulped.

'Thanks, Mr Croakum,' I said.

I raced down the hallway and passed an enchanted mop that lazily sloshed its way about on the tiles. Mum had obviously put it to work earlier that morning.

When I reached the kitchen door, I pushed it open and ducked just in time as a saucepan flew right over my head, knocking the mop clattering across the floor.

Nancy was cooking at the stove like a blur. She was balanced on one leg while her other seven limbs were stirring, whisking, chopping, grabbing spice jars from shelves, flipping ingredients in pans, kneading dough and shoving trays of food into the oven. All at the same time!

'Cockroach purée! Swamp grass! Giblet jam! Unicorn eggs!' she mumbled to herself.

Yep ... that's the kind of food magical creatures like to eat. You get used to it after a while and some of it actually tastes quite good ... I bet you didn't know that unicorns lay eggs?

I darted past Nancy, into the conservatory, and

instantly saw that most of the hotel guests had assembled on the patio outside.

Quickly I made my way along the rows of Mr Croakum and Mrs Venus's plant pots, stepped through the glass door at the far end and . . . a sardine skeleton hit me in the face with a sloppy, smelly **SLAP**.

You weren't expecting that, were you?

Neither was I ...

10

A PRINCELY PARTY

The garden was crowded with guests dressed in their fanciest clothes. Magical creatures can always sniff out a party before it happens.

They were hovering in the air, shuffling round the tables of food that Nancy and Ooof were still busily preparing, huddled on the patio in chattering groups and sitting on the enchanted benches that floated about the flower beds. Hundreds of tiny fairy faces were staring out of the birdhouse-sized boxes that lined the branches of the trees.

I spotted Mum at the foot of the water slide by the pool, frantically talking and gesturing her arms at Mrs Dunch.

Mrs Dunch (Berol to her friends) is a very wrinkly and very, very old mermaid. She's come to stay with us every summer for as long as anyone can remember, and she always insists on squeezing into her starfish bikini top the minute she arrives.

Right then, the geriatric trout was sitting at the top of the slide, listening to Mum's ranting and eating sardines like they were corn on the cob, chewing off all the flesh, then lobbing the skeleton with its head and tail still attached over her shoulder.

That explained my smelly smack in the face.

'Frankie!' Dad yelled from the other side of the patio. 'Will you get over here! You're one of the last to arrive,' he snapped. His shoulders were up near his ears with worry. 'Why are you always late?'

I don't think I'd ever seen Dad looking so smartly dressed. His hair was still messy as usual, but he'd squeezed himself into his old wedding suit. It was moth-eaten and a bit tight in places, but still, that was pretty good for Dad.

He climbed up onto the patio wall, raised his arms and shouted, '**LADIES AND GENTLEMEN!**'

Everyone turned to look at Dad and fell silent.

'LADIES AND GENTLEMEN—'

'And werepoodles,' barked Gladys Potts. She'd put on her special diamond-encrusted collar for the occasion.

'Yes … and werepoodles,' Dad said. 'Now, I called you all here today because—'

'And ghosts!' wailed Wailing Norris. He was another of our ghost guests at the moment. Unfortunately, because Lady Leonora had already booked the great staircase, he'd had to settle for the swimming-pool steps to haunt. He was standing up to his waist in water, shivering dramatically.

'Yes … and ghosts!' Dad said through gritted teeth. 'Now, I—'

'And Cyclopses!' Reginald Blink shouted from further along the patio wall. He was staying with his wife and two children. Their single eyes twitched with excitement.

'Don't forget me!' said another voice from nowhere. For a second no one could figure out where it came from, until a man's toupee wig floated across the lawn.

Invisible Alf had been in a science-laboratory accident when he was young and has been invisible ever since. Even though it's impossible to see him, he's super embarrassed about going bald in his old age and insists on wearing his ratty old wigs. No one really understands why, but it does make it easier to spot him as he dodders about the hotel.

'We haven't forgotten you, Alf,' Dad said.

'Because that would be invisible-ist!'

'Okay.' Dad looked like he might burst into tears. 'Ladies and gentlemen, and werepoodles, and ghosts, and Cyclopses and invisibles—'

'And ogres!'

'And piskies!'

'And mermaids!'

'And impolumps!'

'PLEASE!' Dad practically screamed. 'Everyone. I'm talking to everyone. All. Of. You!'

The crowd fell silent.

'We have a very exciting guest arriving at the hotel today.'

'OOOH, LUMMY!' said the Molar Sisters in unison. They were triplet tooth fairies. Dentina, Gingiva and Fluora. 'Ith it a dentitht?'

It was virtually always impossible to understand what they were saying because they were all missing so many teeth. I bet you didn't know that tooth fairies eat nothing but sugar lumps, did you? They have the worst dental hygiene in the whole of the magical world.

'No, it's not a dentist,' Mum said as she clambered up onto the wall to join Dad.

'How dithapointing. I wath lookin' forward to meetin' a nithe dentitht,' Dentina said.

'It's a goblin prince.' Mum flourished her arms dramatically. 'Prince Grogbah of the Dark and Dooky Deep to be exact.' She was talking with her 'I'm in Charge' voice, and I could see relief spreading across Dad's face now that Mum was taking over.

'We've called you here for a "Welcome, Grogbah" garden party. You're all our guests of honour, and I'm sure you'll be just as thrilled as we are to welcome goblin royalty to the hotel. Let's show Prince Grogbah just how flashy The Nothing To See Here Hotel can be.'

'When is he coming?' came Invisible Alf's voice.

'Well,' Mum said, looking at her watch and frowning, 'he was due about twenty minutes ago.'

'Where ith he then?' moaned the Molar Sisters moaned. 'He'th late!'

'We're all going to die!' screamed Wailing Norris.

Lady Leonora appeared among the crowd and

scowled. She had changed into an extra-wide grey ballgown, and the lacy trim at the bottom wisped and curled round her ankles like smoke.

'Finally I'll have someone of royal blood to talk to,' she said, plucking a ghostly hand mirror out of the air and admiring her reflection. 'I'm *soooo* bored of commoners.'

'I'm so exciterous!' Mrs Dunch cackled, slapping her tail about at the top of the slide.

'My tendrils are twitchy,' said Mrs Venus from her enormous flowerpot. She gnashed her thorn-like teeth and grinned. 'I'm all nervous.'

She wasn't the only one. The prince was nearly half an hour late by now. Everyone was feeling anxious and fidgety, and getting more restless by the minute.

'When's he going to get here?' asked Mum. 'Do you think he's changed his mind?'

'He'll be here,' said Dad, and he was right. It was at that moment that the Lawn started screaming.

THE GOBLINS ARRIVE

The Lawn had been relaxing and snoozing in the middle of the garden for as long as **The Nothing To See Here Hotel** had existed, and most of the time that's all it seemed to be ... just a lawn. But it wasn't. It was an ancient shrubbery sprite. A grassghast.

The only way you might notice something was a little bit odd about the square of grass was the fact that it bunched up into a mound in the middle.

It now began to twitch. Two holes opened up and blinked wildly, followed by a third bigger hole below. A mud-brown tongue suddenly poked out of it. 'Me nethers!' the Lawn hollered.

Everyone turned round and stared. It is a very rare thing to see the Lawn awake. I've lived at the hotel my whole life and I can count on one hand how many times I've seen it open its eyes.

'Oooooh!' The Lawn started squirming about, like there was an earthquake beneath him. 'Someone's messin' with me bumly bits!'

Little molehill-sized lumps of earth started appearing through the grass.

'*Yeooooow!*' the Lawn howled.

'GERROFFF!'

On either side of his mound-head, two grassy, mitten-shaped hands suddenly poked out from beneath the ground.

'That's *eeeeeeeeee-nough*!' The Lawn grabbed at itself like a blanket and yanked the grass on one whole half of the garden aside, exposing the earth underneath. Just in time ... 'BLOOMIN' HOODLUMS!'

BOOOOM!

Mud and dirt flew into the air as a massive, pointy boulder exploded up from underground. It came jutting through the grass at an angle, like the blade of a giant's stone axe. I wish you could have seen it. It was AMAZING!

Little stones and clods of earth rained back down on all of us as everyone gawped in surprise ... and then ... silence.

Nobody moved.

It felt like everyone was holding their breath in unison.

Crick. Crick. Crack.

'What's that noise?' Dad said.

Crackle. Crick. Cruck.

'Wath goin' on?' said the Molar Sisters.

Crick. Crack.

'Door!' Ooof yelled. He'd joined us outside, wearing sunglasses and an enormous straw hat. Ogres don't do well in direct sunlight. It turns them into stone, and it takes ages to loosen them up again. He pointed at the side of the huge boulder. 'Ooof see door!'

'He's right,' said Mum. 'Look!'

We watched as a wide crack made its way across the surface of the rock, tracing out the shape of a huge double door.

'Here we go,' Dad mumbled behind me. 'Hold on to your—'

Suddenly the sound of horns blasted into the air and the doors in the boulder swung wide open.

I nearly fell over when I saw what was on the other side of it. I swear. You wouldn't guess in a squillion years, even if I gave you tons and tons of clues.

Instead of walls of rock and stone, like you'd expect to see on the inside of a dirty great boulder that had just exploded up through your garden, there was a long hallway covered in the brightest, shiniest gold I'd ever seen. Coloured glass lanterns hung on the walls, and everything glinted like the inside of a treasure chest. I had to squint to look along it.

But the gold hallway wasn't even the most impressive thing behind those stone doors because, as far back as I could see, in endless rows like an army, marched hundreds and hundreds of Barrow Goblins.

12

THE PARADE

The first goblin to step out of the giant stone doors was dressed in a yellow silk robe and was dripping in gold. He had dozens of bracelets up his tiny arms and rings on every finger. His skin was papery and blotchy like stale cheese, and his bristly red hair was twisted into a knot on the top of his head.

'Prince Grogbah,' Dad said, stepping out of the crowd and bending down on one knee. 'We are honoured to have you staying with us.'

The little goblin looked up at Dad and grimaced.

'I'm not Grogbah, you noggin-bonked human!' He reached inside his robe and pulled out a gold scroll. 'I am the Royal Shouter.'

'We were exthpecting a printh!' said the Molar Sisters.

'Grogbah will arrive at precisely the right moment,' said the Royal Shouter. He was pulling a face at me, Mum and Dad like we stank.

'Where is he then?' yelled Mrs Dunch from the top of the water slide. She was wriggling and slapping her tail about so much, it was hard to concentrate. 'I want to meet princey-poo!'

'Very tardy if you ask me,' Reginald Blink said. He pulled out a pocket watch and glared at it, tutting.

'Don't you know anything?' the Royal Shouter snapped at everyone. 'A prince never turns up without a parade.'

'A parade? Wat'th that for then?' asked the Molar Sisters.

'If there isn't a parade first, how are you supposed

to know how many subjects the prince has, or how rich and powerful and big and strong and amazerous he is?' The Royal Shouter looked utterly disgusted at our lack of knowledge. 'Now, shut your mumble-holes and let me do my job.'

He unravelled the scroll, planted his feet wide and took a deep breath.

'Presenting,' he bellowed at the top of his tiny voice, 'the Royal Advisors!'

A gaggle of pompous-looking goblins marched out of the doors. Each one was wearing grander robes than the last and, despite only being as tall as my knees, they made me feel nervous.

'The Royal Sorcerers!'

Another gaggle of goblin witches and wizards wobbled out through the doors on tiny sandalled feet. Their robes were covered in strange symbols, and each of the wizards had a beard so long, it dragged along the floor behind him.

'Make way!' they shouted, and threw handfuls of pellets on the ground that exploded with bright red smoke. 'Make way!'

'The Royal Musicians!'

Next came an enormous marching band of goblins holding bizarre-looking instruments, and playing a jazzy tune.

The Royal Shouter introduced jesters, and servants, and chefs, and jugglers, and acrobats. The list seemed endless. He announced a team of goblinette belly dancers who shimmied and jiggled in circles, wearing little jangly tops covered in tiny gold bells. Goblin after goblin after goblin came through the door, but there was no sign of the prince.

'The Royal Pets!'

A group of goblins pulling oversized beetles on leads appeared next. The bugs click-clacked past like shiny black loaves of bread.

'The Royal Back Scratcher!'

He yelled out each goblin's name as they paraded through the doors into the hotel garden.

'The Royal Nose Blower! The Royal Blister Burster! The Royal Earwax Scrubber! The Royal Claw Clipper! The Royal Bath Runner! The Royal Toilet Flusher! The Royal Belly Button Fluff Unflufferer!'

I looked up at Nancy who winked at me and smiled. 'Prince Grogbah thought of everything,' she whispered.

'The Royal Wives!' the little shouting goblin continued as a group of bored-looking goblinettes glided through the doors. Their dresses were a mass of pearls and jewels and feathers, and their hairdos were piled on top of their heads.

'Where are we going to put them all?' Mum whimpered under her breath.

PRINCE GROGBAH

Mum was right to worry. For well over an hour goblins came pouring into the hotel's back garden until there wasn't a bit of space left.

I was starting to believe that the prince didn't exist at all. But finally there was an extra loud horn blast from the musicians.

'Prepare, unworthy creatures,' the Royal Shouter bellowed. 'The time has come for *His Dookiness* to arrive.'

I glanced down the golden corridor and saw an ornate chariot making its way towards us, pulled by a team of miserable-looking goblin servants.

'Heave!' they shouted. 'Heave!'

The chariot reached the double doors, but where was the prince? It seemed to be completely empty, except for a long, thin feather poking up out of it.

I looked about and saw that everyone had the same confused expression on their face. We watched as the feather jiggled, then moved to the edge of the chariot and ... and ... the shortest, fattest goblin I have EVER seen hopped down onto the ground.

Grogbah was barely taller than a bag of flour, but much, much wider. The prince looked like a grey pumpkin in curly-toed slippers. He was dressed in pink and purple robes covered with tiny gold embroidered flowers, and was dripping in jewellery of every kind. Bangles and necklaces tinkled as he walked, and the rings on every one of his fingers glinted in the sunlight. On his head was a bulging turban with a diamond brooch in the shape of a crescent moon on the front, fastening a **HUGE** feather in place. It was five times taller than he was.

'Greetings, pathetic overlings!' he said in a squeaky voice, then smiled as if he'd just paid us all a compliment. 'Bow at my feet. Grovel at My Gobliness.'

'Umm ...' Dad said. He looked back at the rest of us and gestured for us to copy him as he bent down on one knee. We all did the same.

'Lower,' Grogbah commanded. 'Marvel at My Hunkledom.'

We all got onto both knees and bowed forward.

'LOWER OR DIE!'

The goblin guards brandished their swords and bared their teeth.

How were we supposed to bow lower than the prince? We'd have had to lie flat on the ground and shove our faces in the dirt.

'Oh, mighty Grogbah!' Mum blurted out and rushed forward, bowing and nodding like crazy. 'We are so humbled to have you stay at The Nothing To See Here Hotel. On behalf of all of us, staff and guests, we have prepared a—'

'**AAAAAAAGH!**' Grogbah screamed and darted behind the nearest guard. 'Human! There's a human here! A dirty, stupid, lumbering, **UGLY, STINKSOME HUMAN!**'

Mum looked like she'd just been slapped round the chops.

'Prince Grogbah—'

'**AAAAAAAGH!**'

'If I could explain—'

'**AAAAAAAAAAAAGH!**'

'We actually—'

'**AAAAAAAAAAAAGH!**'

'—run the hotel.'

The prince stopped screaming and peeked out from behind the expressionless guard.

'What?' he said. 'Don't lie to me, wretched human! Guards! Slice this human into chunklets and feed her to my beetles.'

'WHOA!' Dad stepped forward and raised his hands. 'It's true, Prince Grogbah. My great-great-grandfather, Abraham Banister, built the hotel.'

The prince reeled backwards when he saw Dad.

'There's more of them,' he said with a look of horror on his little fat face. 'It's a plague!'

'I can assure that there is no plague,' Mum said, trying to sound calm. 'We are the Banister family and we manage this hotel.'

'My great-great-grandmother is Regurgita Glump,' Dad added. He took his glasses off and lifted his head, letting the sunlight catch the copper tinge to his eyes. 'See? I'm a halfling.'

Prince Grogbah stopped his whimpering and glared at both of them. There wasn't a person in the whole of the magical world that hadn't heard of

Granny Regurgita.

'You?' the prince said to Dad. He looked so disgusted, I thought he might be sick. 'The offspring of Mistress Glump?'

'Yep,' Dad replied.

'S'right!' Mrs Dunch shouted from the top of the slide.

'If I may,' Lady Leonora said, floating out of the crowd. She pulled a ghostly flower out of the air and offered it to the prince. 'The Banisters have magical blood and are nothing to worry about, Your Highness.'

'B-but ...' Grogbah's bottom lip trembled.

'We've prepared a feast for you,' Mum said, pulling her famous 'Welcome to the Hotel' smile.

'How could I possibly eat with the **STINK** of humans in the air?'

'There's gull-gizzard pâté and cockroach crostinis,' Nancy said.

Grogbah's jaw dropped and I spotted a little line of drool dribble down his chin. I told you magical creatures were greedy. He stepped back out from behind the guard and straightened his robes.

'Well, I suppose I can tolerate the stink if there's just two humans,' he mumbled.

'Well,' said Mum carefully. 'Actually there are three.'

'WHAT?' Grogbah clutched at his necklaces in panic.

Mum pointed in my direction and the prince slowly shifted his gaze towards me.

'Hello,' I said, waving. I couldn't help but enjoy the look of revulsion on Grogbah's face.

Prince Grogbah blinked wildly, opened his mouth to speak and ... fainted, face down in the mud, with a satisfying

UELCH!

14

A RIGHT ROYAL PAIN

'Hath he popped hith clonkerth?' the Molar Sisters asked.

'If he has, can we eat him?' said Madam McCreedie, the geriatric banshee. She licked her crusty lips hungrily.

Nancy had carried the prince inside, and he was now lying on a sofa in the reception hall, with everyone huddled around. No one knew what to do, so we just stared at him.

Grogbah's subjects and guards and wives seemed very unsurprised that he'd fainted so I guessed this was something he did quite a lot. In fact, for the most part they didn't seem to care at all, and a lot of them had already plodded off for a paddle in the swimming pool.

'He's dead,' shrieked Wailing Norris.

'Don't be ridiculous,' Mum snapped.

'Prince Grogbah?' Dad said, gently poking the little grey lump.

'He's definitely dead,' moaned Wailing Norris.

'NORRIS, WILL YOU SHUT UP!' Mum shot the ghost an angry glare.

'He is!' whimpered the ghost. 'I've never known anyone so dead. With every passing second, that goblin is getting deader and deader. He's the deadest thing I've ever seen!'

'**AAAAAAGH!**' Prince Grogbah screamed

and sat bolt upright on the sofa, as Wailing Norris reeled backwards and sprinted through the nearest wall. 'Where am I?

'Your Highness.' Mum sat down next to the petrified-looking goblin. 'You're in The Nothing To See Here Hotel ... on holiday.'

'Holiday?'

'Yes,' said Nancy. 'You had a little fainting spell when you arrived. Maybe it was all the travelling, or your turban's on a wee bit tight.' She reached down towards Grogbah's red turban with its diamond brooch. 'Let's get this off you, dearie.'

Grogbah recoiled from Nancy as if she was trying to yank off his head.

'No!' he screeched. '**YOU CAN'T HAVE IT!**'

Nancy stopped in her tracks and gawped at the prince with eight wide eyes.

'I'm onto you, you thief! **YOU PIRATE!**' Grogbah pointed a stumpy finger at Nancy. 'You'll never get your filthy hands on my—'

'Turban?' Nancy said.

We all stared. What was the prince talking about?

Had he gone completely potty?

Silence filled the room. Grogbah looked slowly around at all our shocked faces, then lowered his hand and smiled a nervous, wonky smile.

'Haha!' he laughed a bit too loudly. 'Just kidding.'

We all carried on staring.

'Right! Is there anything we can get you?' Nancy asked, breaking the silence. 'Anything at all?'

'Yes,' said Mum, looking flustered. 'We're happy to provide you with anything you wish.'

Grogbah looked about at the dozens of creatures surrounding him, then his face twisted into a pompous, vinegary sneer. He stood up on the cushion he'd been lying on, puffed out his podgy chest and wedged his tiny hands onto his hips.

'I am Prince Grogbah!' he yelled. 'Ruler of the Golden Barrows! Conqueror of the Dooky Deep! And I don't like this grottish, stinksome **SLUM!**'

'Perhaps you'd like us to show you to your room?' said Mum. 'We've saved you our deluxe penthouse. It's got a lovely sea view.'

'No!' shouted the prince. '**NOT GOOD**

ENOUGH! I want this room.'

'This room?' Mum looked like she was about to lay an egg.

'Yes! This room, you prattling pook!'

'But this is the reception hall,' said Dad.

'**DON'T CARE!**' Grogbah shoved a hand in Dad's face. 'I want this one! It's got a high ceiling, and my own private plunge pool.'

'That's the fountain,' Mum explained.

'WRONG!' Grogbah scoffed. 'It's my own private plunge pool. Now, where are my servants?' He clapped his hands. 'Musicians? Dancers! Call the Royal Foot Massager!'

Before Mum and Dad could protest, a gaggle of goblins came running into the reception hall. Musicians gathered on the stone counter and instantly began playing, while others ran to the prince and started cooing and bowing.

'I WANT BEDS!
LOTS OF BEDS!'

More goblins came tripping down the staircase, carrying mattresses above their tiny heads. One or two still had bed sheets on them and folded clothes.

'That's my mattress,' gasped Gladys Potts, pointing at the sheets with a little doggy-bone pattern.

'**HANDS OFF!**' the prince hissed. 'It's mine now. Everything is mine.'

I don't think I've ever been speechless in my life, but, at that moment, I couldn't have spoken even if you'd begged me to. The knobbly little whelp was taking over the entire hotel.

'**YOU!**' Grogbah pointed at Nancy. 'I'm going to take a dip in my plunge pool and I want fresh spider-silk towels. **MAKE THEM! NOW!**'

A battalion of goblin guards surrounded Nancy and pointed their spears and swords at her. Nancy gasped in fright and started frantically weaving large, fluffy towels out of web.

'It would be smart of you all to do exactly as I say, exactly when I say it,' Grogbah announced to the entire room. 'If you want to live, that is ...'

With that, the prince dropped his silk robes to the ground and stood there, BUTT NAKED except for his turban and that stupid feather.

'Well, I never!' the Molar Sisters gasped.

Grogbah strutted towards the fountain, his plump grey bottom jiggling about like a pair of tiny, overboiled chickens.

'**CALL FORTH THE ROYAL BUBBLE BLOWERS!**' Grogbah bellowed as he lowered himself into the fountain.

A team of goblin servants came running into the reception hall, clutching reed-straws in their little hands. They circled the pool below the water-witch statue, dropped to their knees and dipped the ends of their straws into the fountain. Then, taking deep breaths, they started to blow bubbles with every bit of lung power they could muster.

'That's better,' said the prince. 'I almost thought I was going to have to live in squalor on this grotly holiday.'

Just when I thought Prince Grogbah was going to relax and stop barking orders at people, his beady eyes locked onto me. I suddenly felt panicked, so I just shrugged and stared at the floor.

'You! Hideous human child!'

I lifted my head and stared at the nasty little bogey in his bubble bath. The last thing I was going to do was show him I was nervous, even though I was trying very hard not to squirm.

'To the kitchen with you,' Grogbah barked at me. 'Fetch me frog grog. **NOW!**'

I wish I could tell you that I stood my ground and didn't move. I also wish I could honestly say that I shouted, '**GET LOST, YOU CHUBSOME CHUNKER!**' at the prince, but I didn't. Mum and Dad had me well trained to be nice to guests so, before I had time to think, I was halfway to the kitchen ... BUMMER!

PSSST!

I clattered about the kitchen, opening cupboards and pulling out their contents. Where did Nancy keep the frog grog?

Darting up the ladders to the high shelves, I quickly grabbed at the bottles and jars, reading their labels as fast as I could.

It had to be here somewhere.

I clambered back to the floor and was about to dash down the stairs to Ooof's cellar when—

'*Pssst!*'

I stopped in my tracks and looked around the room.

'*Pssst!* Frankie ...'

The yell-a-phone in the corner of the kitchen *DINGED* and the button to Granny Regurgita's room clicked up and down repeatedly.

'Boy? Are you there?'

'Granny?' I ran over to the metal trumpet and put my ear to it. 'Granny, is that you?'

'There you are, youngling,' came Granny Regurgita's voice. 'What's going on down there? My toadstools have been itching all morning. That's always a sign of troubliness.'

'Oh, Granny, it's terrible,' I said. 'Our new guest has only been here for a little while and he's got everyone racing about like slaves.'

'New guest? What new guest?' said Granny.

'Do you remember the goblin messenger out in the storm last night?'

'What about him? Get on with it, you little zit!'

'He brought us a message saying that Prince

Grogbah was coming to stay,' I said. 'He arrived about an hour ago.'

'Prince Grog-who?' Granny grunted.

'Prince Grogbah. He's heir to the throne of the Barrow Goblins.'

'Those underlings,' Granny said. I could picture her grimacing up in her tower. 'What on earth are they doing here? Barrow Goblins never come above the ground, let alone visit a hotel so close to a human town. The smell of people turns their stomachs.'

'He's already made that pretty clear,' I sighed.

'Something's not right,' Granny mumbled.

'Can't you come down?' I asked. There was no way a teeny goblin would mess with the likes of her, even if he was a prince and had an army of guards with curvy swords.

'Abso-BLUNKIN-lutely not!' Granny said. 'I'm snug as a bundle of bugs up here! You all let him in so you can take care of this mess yourselves. Just stamp on the little twerp.'

I groaned into the yell-a-phone as loudly as I could.

'But, boy ...' Granny's voice stopped me just before I turned away. 'Keep an eye out. There's no way Barrow Goblins would come above ground without a very, very good reason. Something sneakerish is going on.'

FROM BAD TO WORSE

After some more frantic searching, I found the bottles of frog grog stashed in a box at the top of the cellar steps, grabbed as many as I could carry and hurried back to the reception hall.

I couldn't get the sight of poor Nancy surrounded by guards out of my head. What had we done, letting a tiny, pumpkin-sized maniac into the hotel?

With any luck, his bubble bath in the fountain would have cheered Grogbah up and he'd be quietly relaxing instead of barking crazy orders at everyone.

I rounded the corner by the dining room, walked through the archway that lead into reception and …

I stopped and gawped at the scene in front of me. How had this happened? I'd only been gone fifteen minutes!

The reception hall was in total chaos. Everywhere I looked, Barrow Goblins were clattering about, upturning furniture and smashing vases.

Dad was standing near a group of lounging goblin-wives, wearing rags just like the other goblin servants. He was holding a fan made from an old broom handle and some sheets of newspaper.

'Waft us, slave!' they snapped at him, with sour expressions. Dad flapped the fan back and forth with a look of complete disbelief on his face.

'*GROOOOOOR!*' Hoggit howled as he scampered past with the Royal Shouter riding on his back. My poor little dragon bucked this way and that to shake the rotten old turnip off, but the Royal Shouter was gripping onto his ears and stayed put.

The dust pooks were rattling across the floor with silver trays of snacks balanced on their heads, and—

'MUM!' I gasped, nearly dropping the bottles of frog grog.

My poor mum was in the middle of the hall, by the fountain with the belly-dancing goblinettes, wearing one of their jingly-jangly tops and skirts. How had they found one to fit?

She looked at me in horror as she tried to copy the dance steps of the other goblin ladies. Mum REALLY took customer service and pleasing guests far too seriously sometimes.

'Don't even think about it, **WHELPLING!**' Grogbah yelled as I darted towards Mum.

I looked up at the goblin prince. He was standing on the top of a pile of torn books from the library, still BUTT NAKED, and brandishing one of Dad's golf clubs.

'What fun!' he laughed, pointing at poor Mr Croakum. A few of the musician goblins had tied the end of his long tongue round the banister rail and were plucking away at it, as if it was the string of a double bass.

'This is the best time I've had in yonkers!' Grogbah said. He swung the golf club over his head, let go of it and cooed with glee as it sailed across the room and smashed through one of the windows by the front door.

It was all too much to take in. Goblins were sliding down the railings of the spiral staircase, and swinging from the lights. One was even throwing darts at the big painting of Great-great-great-grandad Abraham that hung with all the framed reviews above the reception desk.

If they kept this up for much longer, there wouldn't be a hotel left.

It was at that moment that a noise filled the reception hall and every goblin dropped what they were doing and stood still.

A PRINCE ON THE LOOSE

'What's that?' Grogbah said, jumping down from his little mountain of torn books. 'Silence, everyone!'

The reception hall went quiet and we all listened.

Through the smashed window by the front door, the sound of Brighton seafront was floating in. It was such a familiar noise to me that I was almost deaf to it, but the mixture of laughter, music, traffic and seagulls must have been brain-boggling to a Barrow Goblin.

The prince ran to the window and tried to look out. Even on tiptoes he wasn't anywhere near tall enough to see over the windowsill.

'You!' he shouted at the Blink family. 'Here. **NOW!**'

We all watched in painful silence as Prince Grogbah ordered the Blink family onto their hands and knees to make a living, breathing Cyclops stepladder. He then waddled up their backs and peered out through the smashed glass.

'I DON'T BLUNKING BELIEVE IT!' he screamed after a few seconds of staring. 'You lying, cheating, kunkerous **HUMANS!'**

'What's wrong, Your Gobliness?' I said, dumping the bottles of frog grog on the nearest table and running over to the window.

'I've been swizzled!' Prince Grogbah yelled. 'I've been double-crunched!'

'I don't know what you're talking about,' I said. The last thing we needed was to make our grizzly little goblin guest angrier and meaner than he already was.

'Don't know?' Grogbah grabbed me by the chin and pointed straight through the hole in window. 'Don't know, you swindly bamboozle-bonce? Then what's that?'

I followed the line of Grogbah's stumpy finger. He was pointing at the sea.

'THAT'S A MUCH BIGGER PLUNGE POOL THAN MY ONE!' he cried.

'It's the sea—' I began.

'It's mine!' The prince looked like he was about

to have the temper tantrum of the century. 'I want it!'

'YOU CAN'T!' The words just shot out of my mouth. Grogbah gasped in horror. I don't think he'd ever been told he couldn't do or have something in his entire life.

'Can't? **CAN'T???**' His face twisted with anger. **'I AM PRINCE GROGBAH! I WANT THAT BIG, BLUE, GIANT POOL AND I WANT IT NOW!'**

'But it's packed with humans!'

'Humans?' Grogbah said the word like it left a bad taste in his mouth. 'Pah! I'll just order them to **BOG OFF!'**

Before anyone had time to stop him, Grogbah jumped down from the windowsill and, with one big shove of his belly, pushed the front door open and skittered out into the afternoon sunshine.

THE BEACH

'NO!' Mum screamed. She ran across the reception hall, jangling as she went. 'Frankie! Stop him! We can't let people see him!'

I spun back towards the door and saw Grogbah's little naked bottom wobbling down the garden path. In a moment, he'd be through the front gate and out onto the pavement among hundreds of human tourists.

'Quick!' Mum huffed as she darted past me, pinching her nose. Any second the spell on the doorstep would mean her poor human nostrils would be filled with the stench of Brussels sprouts. She hated them!

'Oh no, oh no, oh no!' Dad was hot on Mum's heels. 'He'll blow our cover completely!'

I jumped down the steps onto the front path to see Grogbah pushing open the gate and scurrying through it.

'IT'S MINE!' Grogbah yelled over his shoulder as he hopped across the pavement. There were families strolling in both directions, and traffic for as far as the eye could see. It would take only seconds before he was flattened by a car and we'd all be arrested for Royal Murder ... or worse, he'd be spotted and our secret would be ruined forever.

'Prince Grogbah!' Mum was practically screeching. She reached the gate and hurdled over it like a deranged Christmas decoration.

The prince darted between the legs of two men holding hands and pushing a pushchair. 'HAHA!' he laughed. 'OUT OF MY WAY, PATHETIC HUMANS!'

This was it. The Nothing To See Here Hotel was going to be exposed and we'd be run out of town like monsters.

'**WOOOOOOOOOOOOO!!**' It was Mum. '**WAH-WAH-WEEEEEEEE!**'

Dad and I stopped in our tracks at the gate and stared.

'**YAHOOOOOOOO!**' Mum raised her arms in the air and shimmied. Her jingly-jangly top tinkled loudly as she jumped about. '**OOH-AAH-EEEEE!**'

You genius! I thought to myself. Everyone

on the pavement (including a shocked-looking dog) was gawping at Mum. She whistled and whooped and twirled her way into the road. Cars screeched their brakes, and drivers leaned out of their windows, agog at the BONKERS belly dancer.

'Where is he?' Dad said. 'Quick, while everyone's distracted.'

I scanned the road and pavement on the other side. For a second I thought we'd lost the little twerp, then I caught a glimpse of him waddling out from under an ice-cream van and heading down onto the pebbles.

'He's already on the beach!' I told Dad.

'Oh, this is bad.' Dad grabbed me by the hand and pulled me across the road.

My eyes darted back and forth, trying to spot Grogbah. Normally the beach was only filled with old people snoring in their deckchairs on weekday afternoons, but I could already see a big group of children on a school trip heading towards us in the distance ... and ...

'AAAAGH!' Dad spotted them too. Way ahead of us, too far to catch him, Grogbah was skittering straight towards the big class of kids. I couldn't hear what he was shouting, but he was waving his stumpy arms, so I guessed he was ordering them to get away from his plunge pool.

'We're done for,' Dad said.

'Think of something!' Mum yelled as she caught

up with us. 'There has to be a—'

'HELLO, DARLINGTH!' We spun round, and standing right behind us were three very old men in crumpled suits. Each of them had an enormous white beard and gappy, rotten teeth.

'Ummm,' Mum said. 'I'm sorry, we haven't got time to—'

'It'th uth,' the three men said in unison. 'The Molar Thithterth.'

'The Molar Sisters!?' Dad gasped.

They each pulled a magic wand from one of their crumpled suit pockets and winked.

'We haven't played with a thpot of magic in yonkth.'

Mum looked like she was about to cry. 'You brilliant, brilliant men ... ladies ... men ...'

'Where ith the little blighter?' said the sisters.

Dad pointed at Grogbah who was only a few seconds away from running head first into the schoolchildren and blowing the secret of the hotel for good.

'Oh, blunkin' bunionth!' the Molar Sisters said when they spotted the prince. 'We need to clear thith beach, quick.' With that, they mumbled a few odd-sounding words under their breath and gave a violent flick of their wrists.

I'd never seen tooth fairies casting spells before, but it wasn't quite as impressive as I'd hoped. One

of their wands snapped as they flicked it, and another let go of hers and lobbed it into the sea.

'That ought to do it.'

'What ought to do it?' said Mum after a few seconds. 'What did you actually do?'

'Jutht you watch,' the Molar Sisters said, grinning proudly.

Suddenly the pebbles on the beach seemed to lurch under our feet, and the air was filled with a strange crunching sound. 'Look,' Dad said and pointed at the ground. All of the pebbles were jumping and jostling about. Then, one by one, they sprouted legs and little eyes on stalks. Before we knew it, Brighton beach had been replaced by millions and millions of tiny hermit crabs. They scuttled about, and tumbled over each other.

'Ugh!' Mum yelped. 'They're disgusting!'

'Exactly,' said Dad. 'YOU DID IT!' He scooped the three old men into a bear hug.

Dad was right. I looked along the beach and saw all the human tourists screaming and running for the safety of the pavement at the top of the swarm of crabs. The Molar Sisters had cleared the beach before anyone could spot Prince Grogbah, who was now flailing about, kicking and swatting at the little creatures.

'Ooof here to help,' came another voice from behind us. Ooof was still wearing his massive straw hat and sunglasses, and had wrapped himself in one of Mum's sarongs from the kitchen laundry pile. It was a pretty convincing disguise.

'Get him, QUICK!' Dad said, pointing at the prince.

'Ooof grab Grog!' Ooof shouted, and loped off across the crabs. Then, just when I thought the ogre would snatch Grogbah off his feet, Ooof jumped into the air and came crashing down on top of him, wrestling the prince flat.

'Got him!' Ooof shouted, waving back at us. 'Grogbah grabbed.'

THE PLOT THICKENS

Wow! We've made it to CHAPTER NINETEEN! It's a good story, isn't it? Well, don't go anywhere just yet because it's almost time for the big, **MASSIVE**, climactic plot twist. All the best stories have one ...

Prince Grogbah was in a foul mood by the time we'd all raced back across the crab-infested beach and got him safely into the hotel.

Ooof dropped him in the middle of the reception-hall floor, and everyone stepped away, eyeing him nervously. Grogbah's goblin subjects and the other guests were crowded up the great staircase. They'd been watching at the windows and saw the whole fiasco unravel.

'I HATE YOU!' Grogbah finally screeched

when he'd clambered back to his feet. 'This is the *worst* HOTEL IN THE WORLD!'

'Oh dear,' said the three old men in crumpled suits, as their features melted back to those of the Molar Sisters. 'What a thulky tho-and-tho.'

Two of the prince's slaves ran forward and helped him get dressed back into his golden robes, and Nancy approached with a glass of frog grog.

'Maybe a wee tipple will cheer you up?' she said.

Prince Grogbah snatched the glass and hurled it at the wall. 'You think I want to drink anything in this **HONK HOLE?**' he screamed in Nancy's face.

If the prince's face wasn't greyish-green, I'd swear he was turning purple with rage. It was quite something to watch.

'If I'd known I'd have to deal with **THIS!**' Grogbah shouted, gesturing around the room. 'Commoners, and peasants, and humans ... **I NEVER WOULD HAVE CHOSEN TO HIDE OUT HERE!**'

Grogbah realised what he had just said and clamped his little hands over his mouth.

MAGICALS WELCOME!
THE NOTHING to see HERE HOTEL
BRIGHTON, UK

'What?' said Mum. 'Did you just say—'

'NOTHING!' The Royal Shouter ran forward and stood between us and Grogbah. 'The prince didn't say anything. We're not hiding out! Who said anything about hiding out?'

'Yes ... erm ... I mean ... we're just having a winksy little holiday,' Grogbah said, laughing nervously. 'We're definitely not on the run and I'm certain that I didn't steal anything from a rival clan of goblins who are now after us.'

Grogbah stared at us all with wide eyes.

'You little criminal!' Dad said, rolling up his sleeves and trying to look tough. 'You come into my family's hotel, then insult us, humiliate us, wreck the place and nearly blow our secret **BECAUSE YOU'VE BROKEN THE LAW?**'

'Now can we eat him?' said Madam McCreedie.

'Ooof squish him,' said Ooof, raising a huge foot in the air.

Grogbah's eyes looked like they were about to pop out of his skull. He looked at the Royal Shouter, then at the gaggle of us standing around him, then back to the Royal Shouter.

'Ummm ...' he said. '**GUARDS! ARREST EVERYONE!**'

And they did ...

There was nothing we could do. Goblin weapons are sharp, you know.

By the time night fell, we'd all been sitting about for hours. The little pouting pumpkin's guards surrounded us with their spears and made every non-goblin sit on the floor in the middle of the room.

Things were looking pretty hopeless, but you'll be glad to know it didn't end there.

I bet you're wondering just who Grogbah had stolen something from, aren't you? I know I was. It's all I could think about.

Well ... you're about to find out.

We were all sitting in silence, except the prince. He was hunched over a little table, noisily scoffing the remains of Nancy's garden feast, when it happened.

I was sitting on the floor, bored, with a numb

bottom, and I had no idea ... not a clue ... not the tiniest inkling that everything was about to go

WHOOMMFF!!

The *WHOOMMFF*-iest *WHOOMMFF* I'd ever seen or heard!

WHOOMMFF!

WHOOOOOOOOOOOOOOOO

The front door exploded inwards and a huge, rusty cannonball arced across the reception hall and wedged itself in the wall just above the painting of Great-great-great-grandad Abraham.

'NOBODY MOVE!' a voice shouted. I couldn't be exactly sure as my ears were ringing from the blast, but it sounded like the voice of a girl. It was coming from the front steps, but it was dark and there was so much smoke and dust that no one could see who it belonged to. 'OR ELSE!'

Nobody moved a muscle. Even Prince Grogbah quickly sprawled himself across the table, stunned into silence.

I stared with wide eyes as the dust cloud rolled through the hole in the wall where the front door used to be.

'What was that, First Mate Plank?' a second voice in the smoke asked. It was high-pitched and scratchy, like the hinges on the back garden gate.

OOOOOOOOOOOOMMFF!

'I said—' came the girl's voice.

'Eh?' asked the scratchy voice.

'Will you SHUT UP!' the girl's voice snapped. 'You're ruining my entrance! And, while we're at it, I hadn't said FIRE yet.'

'What?'

'I hadn't given the command!'

'What command?'

'FIRE!' The girl was clearly losing her temper. I could hear the sound of her stamping on the spot. 'I HADN'T SAID FIRE!'

'Oh!' the scratchy voice said. 'FIRE!'

There was another enormous **WHOOMMFF** and a second rusty cannonball shot through the hole in the wall and demolished the cloakroom door.

'Oh, forget it!' the girl's voice shouted. There was the sound of footsteps and a silhouette suddenly appeared in the smoke.

Prince Grogbah obviously recognised the little shape as he started mumbling, '*NO, NO, NO,*' under his breath.

The girl emerged into the reception hall and stood, feet wide apart with her hand on her hip. She aimed a tiny musket into the air and fired it.

'My name is Tempestra Plank!' she yelled. 'And I've come to reclaim our treasure.'

'I'm out of 'ere!' yelled one of Grogbah's guards. He dropped his spear and ran out of the room.

'Me too!' blubbed another.

'And me.'

'*Oooooh-ho-ho!*' the Molar Sisters cooed together, clapping their hands with excitement. In a moment, most of the prince's guards had abandoned their posts. The remaining few lowered their weapons and watched in horror.

'Ha!' Tempestra laughed. I'd never seen a creature like her in real life. She was obviously a goblin, but a completely different species to Prince Grogbah and his Barrow cronies. I'd read about her kind in some of Grandad Abraham's books. Squall Goblins! Voyagers that sailed the deepest sewers and oceans and who NEVER came ashore. Whatever Grogbah had stolen, it must have been very valuable.

Where the Barrow Goblins were short and round, Tempestra was tall and slim. If she'd stood next to me, she would easily be as high as my shoulder. Her curly red hair was wedged under a tricorne hat, and she was wearing a long peacock-blue coat with ruddy boots that laced all the way up to her knees.

'Where's Grogbottom?' she said through gritted teeth.

Everyone sitting on the floor pointed at Prince Grogbah, who was tiptoeing his way towards the nearest exit. The prince froze and turned to face the goblin girl, laughing nervously.

Tempestra's eyes lit up with vengeful glee when she saw Grogbah in the crowd.

'AVAST, SEWER RATS!' she shouted, and ... well ... I swear to you that I'm not lying ...

The hull of a goblin pirate ship came CRASHING through the wall. Guests and goblins alike scattered in all directions as huge chunks of the staircase fell inwards and shattered on the black and white tiles.

Seawater splashed round our ankles as the enchanted wave that had carried the ship up the beach hit its mark.

RAAAAGH!

The ship's pirate crew clambered down the wooden sides or swung to the ground on ropes. They were a terrifying bunch of goblins and goblinettes. Some of them wore eyepatches or had peg legs or hooks for hands, and all of them were brandishing cutlasses.

'Get him!' Tempestra ordered, and her crew rushed at the prince. They grabbed him and dragged the chubby goblin, kicking and flailing, towards the girl.

'I can explain!' Prince Grogbah yelled. 'I only borrowed it!'

'PREPARE TO DIE!' Tempestra hissed in the prince's face, drawing a sword from her belt.

Everyone grimaced and squinted. Everyone except Mum.

'**HOLD IT!**' she bellowed. The entire hall stopped what they were doing and turned to stare. 'WHAT'S GOING ON? YOU CAN'T JUST BLOW A HOLE IN OUR HOTEL, THEN MURDER A GUEST IN RECEPTION. EVEN IF GROGBAH IS A LOATHSOME

LITTLE TOAD!'

Suddenly my brain caught up with everything that was happening and my jaw fell open. I looked at the pirate girl. I looked at the ship. I looked at the crew, and I knew I'd seen them before. My brain started racing. What did Tempestra say her last name was?

I nearly fell over with excitement.

'Plank!' I gasped. I was staring at the daughter of the greatest goblin pirate that ever lived.

'Captain Calamitus Plank!'

BONES IN A BOX

Tempestra smiled at me, then looked back at Mum.

'Sorry, Madam.' She removed her tricorne hat and bowed low, then turned and poked a slender finger into the end of Grogbah's nose. 'We've been searching for this grottish little blunker for years.'

'Why?' Mum said with a quivering voice. 'Who are you?'

The pirate girl tucked her sword back into her belt, then reached up, grabbed Mum's hand and shook it.

'I am Tempestra Plank, First Mate on board the *Blistered Barnacle*,' she said, pointing back at the ship. 'The boy's right: my father is Captain Calamitus Plank, the Skurge of the Seven Sewers. This slug dropping—' she pointed at Prince

Grogbah '—stole his most precious treasure, and we've come to takc it back.'

Everybody oohed and aahed. There wasn't anyone in the magical world that hadn't heard of the wild adventures of Captain Plank.

'Let me go!' Grogbah yelled, wriggling in the clutches of the pirate crew. 'On second thoughts, I really don't know what you're chittering on about. I haven't got anything that belongs to you.'

'Where are they?' Tempestra snapped.

'Haven't got a clue!'

'WHERE ARE MY FATHER'S DIAMONDS?'

'Never heard of them,' Grogbah spluttered.

'TELL US!'

The prince started squirming and twisting even harder so that the pirates struggled to keep hold of him.

'I'LL NEVER TELL!' Grogbah screamed, just as he jerked sideways and stepped into a shaft of moonlight that was slanting through the hole in the reception wall.

Suddenly the room was filled with hundreds of tiny stars as something near the prince's head reflected the moonbeam in every direction.

'Aha!' Tempestra marched over to Grogbah and yanked the brooch off the front of his turban. 'GOT THEM!'

'No! MY DIAMONDS!' Grogbah whined as his enormous feather drooped and fell to the floor.

'Stop snivelling!' one of the crew members said to Grogbah as he tied up the prince's hands and feet.

Tempestra held the little treasure up to the light, and for the first time I saw that it wasn't a crescent-moon-shaped brooch at all; it was a pair of diamond-encrusted false teeth!

'Go and get Dad,' Tempestra said to her crew, and two pirates ran back to the ship and climbed onboard.

Moments later they reappeared on the deck, lugging a wooden chest. 'HEAVE-HO!' they chanted together and threw the box down to the other crew members.

'Wait a minute,' my dad said, scratching his head.

'Captain Plank is in there?'

'Yes,' said Tempestra.

'In a treasure chest?'

'Yep.'

'Well, let him out,' Dad said, looking star-struck. He was a huge fan of the captain's stories, just like me. 'It must be very uncomfortable. Would he like some tea?'

Tempestra lifted the lid and everyone crowded round to look inside the box.

'OH MY GOODNESS!' Mum gasped.

'He'th very thkinny,' the Molar Sisters said.

'He looks delicious,' said Gladys Potts. She instantly sprouted fluffy white fur and turned into a poodle.

I pushed through the huddle of guests, reached the edge of the wooden chest and looked inside.

'It's ... it's ...' I said.

'It's just bones.' Dad finished my sentence.

Had the crew of the *Blistered Barnacle* gone mad? Why on earth were they chasing Prince Grogbah for all this time, when their captain was a skeleton? Not even a skeleton really ... just a *pile* of bones, with a toothless skull sitting on top.

'Why do you think we needed the diamond dentures?' Tempestra said. 'Watch!'

She reached inside the chest and carefully placed the glittering teeth into the skull's mouth.

'*BLAAAARG!*' Quicker than a firework, the bones reassembled and we suddenly found ourselves staring into the empty eye sockets of a goblin skeleton, standing waist-high in a treasure chest.

'Oh, I feel like I've been bonejangled!'

'What?' I said. 'This isn't right.' My brain started racing again. In my books, Captain Plank was a goblin with hair and skin and eyes. Not a skel—

'Dad!' Tempestra threw her arms round the skeleton and roughly hugged it.

Pffft! The skeleton spat the teeth back out in surprise and hundreds of little bones clattered back into the box.

Tempestra turned to face us with Captain Plank's skull in her hands.

'Ooops ...' she said, rolling her eyes. 'See? This happens A LOT!'

She bent down, picked the diamond dentures up off the floor and placed them back between Calamitus's jaws.

'Wha-what?' The bones were instantly a skeleton again. 'Blimey, I've got a headache.'

'Dad!' Tempestra said again. 'Welcome back!'

'Eh?' Captain Plank looked at his daughter. 'Back? Where've I been?'

The skeleton turned its head and noticed us all crowding round the treasure chest he was standing in.

'Hello,' Mum said.

'We're thrilled to have you here,' Dad joined in.

'Who are you?' Captain Plank croaked. 'What's going on?'

Tempestra tapped Calamitus on his bony shoulder, then pointed to a mirror that was hanging on the nearby wall.

The captain swivelled round to look at his reflection and stared for a moment. It's very hard to guess the emotions of a skeleton. Who knew eyebrows were so important?

'Oh, blunkers. I'd forgotten about the bone thing,' he said.

Just then a small growl from somewhere up above caught our attention. It wasn't a very loud growl, but it echoed off the broken walls and even Captain Plank looked about, clacking his teeth.

I turned and glanced up to the first-floor landing, where the huge chunk of staircase had been smashed away. There, curling its little toes over the edge, was Gurp.

'Gurp!' Mum said. 'What are you doing down here?'

Clomp, clomp, clomp, clomp!

Something very large, and very heavy, was coming down the stairs from high above.

'Oh no,' said Dad.

Clomp, clomp, clomp, clomp!

'Oh dear,' Nancy mumbled under her breath. 'I

think all this noise might have woken your—'

'**WORST NIGHTMARE!**' Granny Regurgita rounded the last twist of the spiral staircase and grimaced down at us. She didn't say anything else at first, and just looked about at the smashed front door, tied-up goblin prince, skeleton standing in a treasure chest and pirate ship sticking through the wall. Then she fixed her copper eyes on me, Mum and Dad.

'Someone's got a whopsy load of explaining to do ...'

THE CURSE OF THE DIAMOND DENTURES

'Granny Regurgita,' Dad said. 'Granny ... I can explain ...'

'Go on then, Bargeous, you snivelling little dollop of **SNOT!**' Granny said. (Believe it or not, that's one of the nicest things she's ever said to Dad.)

'Well ...' Dad started sweating. 'Ummm ... There were crabs ...'

'Crabs?' Granny raised one bristly eyebrow.

'Yes. And ... umm ... a big boom in the garden ... and Gladys Potts's mattress.'

'Go on.'

'And skinny-dipping ... that ship over there ... oh ... and the Lawn screamed.'

Granny Regurgita was gawping at Dad like he'd gone round the twist.

'Phew,' Dad said, smiling with relief. 'Now it's all much clearer, no?'

I'd never seen my granny looking lost for words before.

'Ahem!' Calamitus Plank stepped out of the treasure chest and walked forward. 'I think I might be able to clear this whole messy thing up.'

'Who are you?' Granny grunted.

'Oh, come on, Regurgita. You know me.' The skeleton smiled a flashy, diamond smile.

'I've NEVER clapped my peepers on you in my life!'

'What's the matter?' Captain Plank chuckled. 'Don't you recognise old Calamitus without his skin?'

Granny Regurgita gasped and well … I think she might even have smiled.

'Calamitus Plank, is that you, you old sea slug?'

'The very same.' The skeleton gave a little bow.

Granny scooped Gurp up in her massive arms and jumped off the broken staircase. She landed with an enormous **THUMP** that made the ground shake.

'What have you done to yourself?' she asked, putting Gurp down on the wet floor. 'Where's all your podge, and your skin, and your …' she paused, 'face?'

'It's a long story,' Calamitus said, scratching bony fingers against the top of his skull with an ear-bursting squeak. 'I told a sea witch I loved her.'

'Oh, how lovely,' Nancy said.

'It was,' Calamitus continued. 'The trouble was I also told a mermaid I loved *her*.'

'Oh, that'th never a good idea,' the Molar Sisters joined in.

'S'right,' Calamitus said, shaking his head. 'My witchy love found out and – **FLASH, CRACKLE** – I'm a walking skeleton with magical teeth that everyone wants to steal. Magpies are a nightmare.'

'But how does that explain all this mess?' Granny said, shuffling about, surveying the damage.

Everyone turned and stared at Prince Grogbah, who had been tied up with so much rope, he looked like more like a ball of wool than a goblin.

'Don't look at me, peasants!' he spat.

'Him,' Tempestra said, striding up next to her father and pointing at the goblin prince.

'Tempestra Plank,' Granny said, eyeing the pirate girl. 'Last time I saw you, you were squincier than a skwabling.'

'It's been a long time,' Tempestra said. 'Most of it has been spent with Dad in a box, searching for this thieving goblin prince.'

'The last thing I remember,' Calamitus said, 'we were sailing through a sewer that led right through the Dooky Deep. I'd toddled over to the railing of me ship, you know, to do me business over the side, and a bunch of Grogbah's cronies grabbed me and nabbed me dentures before I could even take a tinkle.'

'And you've been on the run ever since?' Dad asked Grogbah.

'You should be ashamed of yourself!' said Mum.

'I couldn't help it,' the prince snapped back. 'The diamonds were really shiny. I like shiny things. **I WANT SHINY THINGS!**'

'Well, what's to be done now?' Granny Regurgita said. 'Everyone knows it's goblin law that a wrong can only be righted by a BLUNKIN' BIG BATTLE!'

'I'm quite tired,' Calamitus said. He flexed his arms and they cracked loudly. 'Do we have to?'

But Prince Grogbah yelled, '*GUARDS!*' and the huge reception hall suddenly filled with Barrow Goblins. They hadn't run off at all! Those sneaky little blighters had gone to round up the rest of the troops, knowing that they would need to fight the pirates! Grogbah's army came pouring out of the dining room and from the garden; there was even a battalion waiting on the stairs with their spears raised and ready.

Granny Regurgita looked at Calamitus and winked. 'I think that answers your question,' she said.

GET 'EM!

All at once, Grogbah's guards flew into action. They darted towards the prince to untie him, while others started charging at us, swinging weapons above their heads.

'**OH NO YOU DON'T!**' Granny Regurgita bellowed. She ploughed into the horde of goblin soldiers like a demented rhinoceros, sending pumpkin-sized bodies flying into the air. '*RAAAGH!*'

Calamitus tripped a passing guard and snatched his sword in mid-air. 'Let's see if there's life in me old bones yet.'

I looked at Mum, who nodded at me, then grabbed an umbrella from the hatstand and threw it.

'**LET 'EM HAVE IT, FRANKIE!**'

she yelled over the din as she picked up a mop and

whacked a goblin in the face with it. In no time at all, the hotel was a mass of flailing limbs, jabbing spears and bits of furniture flying through the air.

'HOOLIGANS!' Lady Leonora exploded a jet of ectoplasm into the faces of three snarling soldiers.

'*AAAAAEEEEEEE!*' A goblin guard sailed past my head and landed in the fountain with a huge splash.

'Take that!' I turned round just in time to see Tempestra Plank shoot one of the chandeliers, which came crashing down on a gaggle of goblin heavies.

It was dizzying to take in.

Nancy had clambered up the wall and was shooting great nets of spiderweb at unsuspecting guards, then hoisting them into the air.

'Don't you think you'll get away with this!' she shouted at the little wriggling soldiers.

I ran towards the fountain, batting guards aside with my umbrella, trying to get a better view of the room. I'd nearly made it when I had to hurdle Gladys Potts as she scampered past with a broom handle between her teeth, tripping goblins left and right.

OOOH! AAGH! EEEK! UHFF!

The battle was now raging all over the place, but all I could think of was Grogbah. Where had the rotten whelp gone? I had to find him!

'FRANKIE!' I heard Dad's voice yell.

I turned round and almost burst out laughing at what I saw. There Dad was with the vacuum cleaner nozzle aimed right on the top of the Royal Shouter's head. The little twerp's knot of red hair had been sucked up, and he was thrashing about like a fish on the end of a hook.

'THAT WAY!' Dad pointed at the library. '**GROGBAH WENT THAT WAY!**'

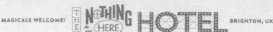

I sprinted towards the library, ducking under one of Grogbah's henchmen as he shook about in mid-air. For a second I thought it was magic, until I noticed the ratty toupee in front of him. 'Ha! Good on you, Alf!' I shouted.

When I reached the archway to the library, I stopped and watched with a mixture of shock and delight as a squad of goblin swordsmen were pelted with books by the dust pooks, who were hurling them at a surprising speed for potato-sized little chunks.

But where was the prince?

On the other side of the library, Madam McCreedie was swatting at some of Grogbah's sour-faced wives with a feather duster. The wives were whipping back at her with the long strings of pearls that dangled off their fancy gowns.

'**OH, I'M GETTING BORED OF THIS!**' screeched Madam McCreedie, then let rip a banshee wail so loud that the wives were bowled backwards and straight through the wall into the kitchen. '**AND DON'T COME BACK!**'

For a second all I saw through the hole were scurrying feet and smashing plates, but then I caught a glimpse of pink robes with tiny gold embroidered flowers hurrying past.

'Gotcha!' I said to myself. I ran to the hole in the wall and ducked down to look through it.

Sure enough, there was the prince, waddling along the edge of the kitchen to avoid all the fighting, then ducking into the conservatory. But I knew he wasn't going to stop there.

Grogbah was heading for the garden.

WHERE IS GROGBAH?

I raced towards the kitchen.

Why hadn't I thought of it before? If the prince made it to the garden, he'd escape back through the boulder he'd arrived in and get away with EVERYTHING!

The kitchen was just as chaotic as the rest of the hotel.

'Take that! And thith!' The Molar Sisters were clutching their wands and had conjured up a tornado of plates and cups in the middle of the room. Cutlery and all kinds of jars, pans and utensils whizzed past, bouncing off the cupboards and shelves, and pelting the Royal Sorcerers.

The ancient goblin wizards chanted spells and threw their smoke pellets, but they didn't stand a chance against the tooth fairy triplets.

'You call that magic?' Dentina laughed over the tornado.

'Ha!' Gingiva laughed. 'Nonthenth!'

'Your beardth look marvellouth in the wind though,' Fluora added, grinning.

I ran into the kitchen and barged straight past the Royal Sorcerers, knocking them stumbling across the room.

'STOP!' a wheezy voice croaked. I turned just in time to see a grizzled goblin wizard in his biscuit-tin-sized wheelchair careering towards me. 'I'LL GET YOU, YOU SNOTLING!'

'Oh, thtop your madneth!' the Molar Sisters laughed. They flicked their wands and I flew into the air, just as the old grunion sped underneath me and clattered down the steps to Ooof's basement. 'Where to, thweety?' they cackled, dancing about in their magical storm.

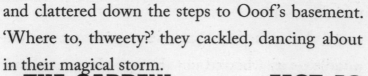

'**THE GARDEN!**' I hollered. '**FAST AS YOU CAN!**'

The Molar Sisters swatted their wands in my direction, and the tornado of crockery suddenly wrapped itself round me.

Fast as a rocket, I flew straight through the door to the conservatory and hurtled above the rows of Mr Croakum's flowers, ferns and huge mushrooms in plant pots.

Below me, running this way and that, I saw Tempestra's pirate crew beating back a gaggle of goblin guards. Most of them had lost their weapons by now and were just hurling gardening tools at each other, but I was pleased to see that it looked like the pirates were winning.

I reached the far end just in time to see Reginald Blink throw a potted cactus at a small running figure dressed in gold, darting through the door to the garden. It was Grogbah! I'd nearly caught up with him.

As the tornado of crockery (with me in the middle of it) whizzed out through the end of the conservatory, the Molar Sisters' spell instantly vanished and I skidded onto the mound at the centre of the Lawn with plates and cups smashing all around me.

'***Uuuuurgh!***' The Lawn woke up for the second time in twenty-four hours.

'Sorry,' I huffed. I felt like I'd just been put through a long spin in a tumble dryer. I dizzily stood up and looked about. There was no way I was going to let the prince escape.

'You're standing on my face!' the Lawn grumbled. '**GERROFF!**'

I wobbled down the mound and headed for the bare patch of mud with the boulder jutting out of it. *Please let the door still be closed! PLEASE LET THE DOOR STILL BE CLOSED!*

Phew! It was. Prince Grogbah may have made it as far as the garden, but he hadn't got through into the golden hallway yet and, if I stayed near the boulder, he wouldn't be able to open the door without dealing with me first.

I squinted my eyes and peered into the towering flower bed, searching for a pumpkin-shaped figure. It was at times like this that I loved having troll blood in my veins. Seeing in the dark was a piece of cake, except the brilliant, glowing petals and leaves that burst out in all directions only made the shadows between them seem even darker.

I couldn't spot the prince, but I knew he'd probably spotted me. I needed to be ready—

'***GROOOOR!***'

I spun round and gasped. Up on the patio, I saw Hoggit struggling and thrashing about as two of Grogbah's royal guards had lashed ropes round the little dragon's snout and were pulling him towards the swimming pool.

NOOOOOOOOOOOO!!!! I'm sure you've probably guessed by now, but soot-dragons die if they get wet!

I didn't have a choice. Abandoning my post at the boulder door, I sprinted across the garden and leaped up the patio steps. I don't think I'd ever been so angry in my life. I could feel Granny Regurgita's troll rage bubbling up inside by belly.

'GET AWAY FROM HIM!' I bellowed. **'THAT'S MY DRAGON!'**

I grabbed the two soldiers by their red topknots and yanked them off the ground. They dropped the ropes and started kicking their stumpy legs.

'Let go!' they squeaked. 'LET GO!'

'Up here, darling!' Mrs Dunch shouted. She was clambering up the steps of the water slide. 'Throw 'em!'

One after another, I swung the goblins into the air.

'AEEEEEEEEEE!'

They arced up over the pool and Berol Dunch batted them with her fishtail with a loud, wet *SLAP!*

I couldn't help feeling a bit sorry for the goblin guards when they both landed head first in the manure pile by the potting shed, but that's what you get for messing with Frankie Banister. Haha!

And that was the moment everything went *really* crazy.

GRUNCHED

Brace yourself: we've arrived at the big CLIMACTIC ending of the story. Ready? You sure? Okay, here we go ...

I pulled the ropes off Hoggit's snout and bent down to pick him up. The poor little thing was trembling with fear and whimpering quietly.

'It's okay, buddy,' I said, stroking his scaly head. 'You're safe now.'

Bundling him under my arm, I stood up to see Grogbah making a run for it across the Lawn.

'You'll NEVER get me, you ranciderous peasant!'

As if the magic doors had sensed Grogbah was getting close, they began to creak open.

'You actually thought a squivelling skrunt like you could defeat a hunksome prince like me?'

The door opened further. In a few seconds, it would be too late.

I was about to jump over the patio wall and try my luck at catching up with Grogbah, when I noticed Hoggit was getting really hot under my arm.

I looked down and saw a fierce glow coming from between his lumpy scales. My little pet began to vibrate and a rumbling sound echoed out through his open mouth.

Then, for the first time ever, Hoggit let rip the most tremendous spray of fire I'd ever seen. It exploded through the air and engulfed the boulder completely.

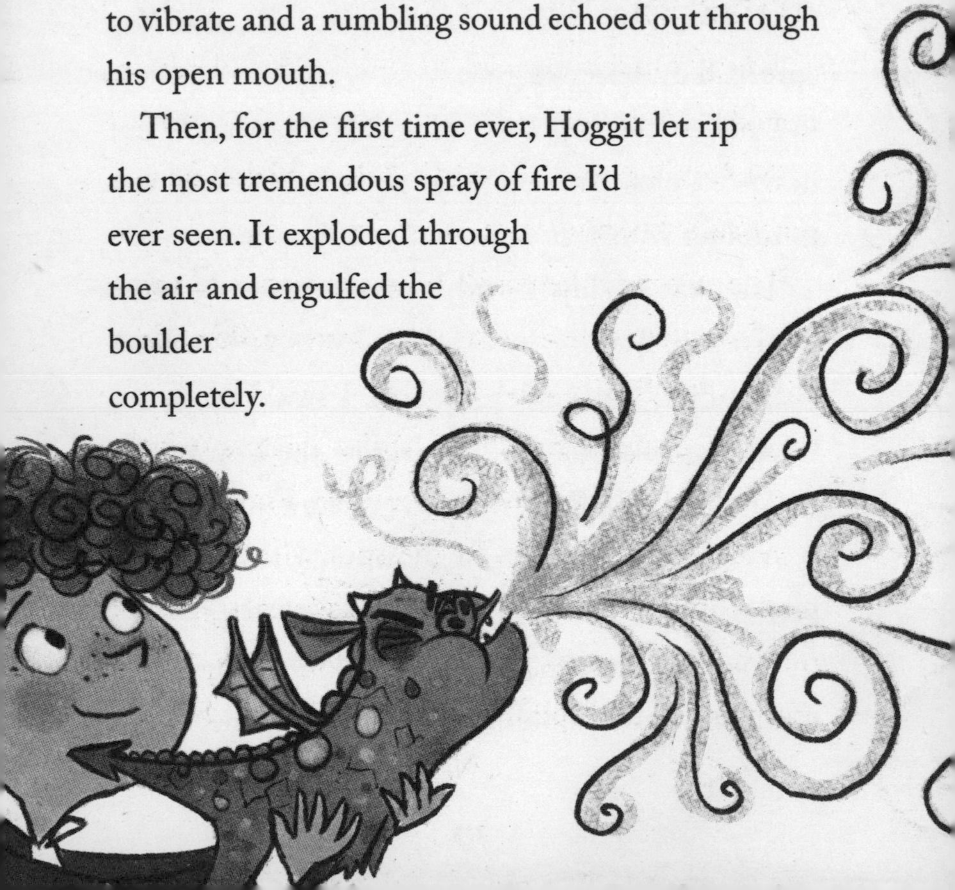

Grogbah screamed and reeled backwards.

'What's going on?' Mum cried, running out of the conservatory.

'Hoggit!' Dad yelled as he joined her.

I couldn't turn round with Hoggit shooting fire though the air, but I could hear the sounds of the hotel guests and the pirate crew assembling behind me.

'LOOK AT HIM GO!' Calamitus shouted. 'STUPENDOUS!'

'Keep Hoggit aimed in the right direction, Frankie,' Mum told me.

'Melt that boulder!' said Dad. I could feel he was practically hopping with excitement.

The night air began to fill with a sour burning smell as the boulder started to glow yellow, then purple, and finally white.

'It'th gonna blow!' the Molar Sisters wailed together. 'Thizzle it good and proper, Frankie!'

Grogbah was frozen to the spot with a look of terror on his face. He watched as great globs of molten rock started pouring down the sides of his escape route and splashing on the scorched earth.

'Hath anyone got any marthmallowth?' the Molar Sisters continued, as …

BLOP! BLUB! GLOOOP! PLOP!

A huge gurgling sound erupted from beneath the boulder and it sank into the ground, oozing back the way it had come in a tremendous lava flow.

There was silence for a moment, until all eyes slowly turned to Grogbah.

The toady little sneak had his mouth hanging open like he was trying to catch flies. Then he glanced up and saw the patio was crowded with guests and goblin pirates and he jolted back to his senses.

'I … I …' Grogbah glared at me. He looked like he was about to be sick with rage. '**I HATE YOU! I HATE ALL DIRTISH, PUTRID, PUFFY-FACED, SPINE-JANGLED, WEAKLY, COMMONOUS, MUCKSOME, *STUUUUUPID* HUMANS! BUT I ESPECIALLY HATE YOU!**'

One of the goblin guards that Mrs Dunch had

whacked across the garden had dropped his sword as he flew through the air. It was sticking up out of the edge of the flower bed, and Grogbah made a lunge for it.

'I'M GOING TO POKE HOLES IN YOU AND YOUR MANKSOME LITTLE DRAGON AND USE YOU AS A TEA-STRAINER!' the prince screamed at me.

'Not so fast.' Calamitus hopped over the patio wall, down to the Lawn.

'Ain't you forgetting something, Prince Grog-Bog?' said Granny. She lumbered down the patio steps and joined Captain Plank.

The prince sneered at them both.

'The bristly battle has been fought and won, and now, as is the goblin way, it's time for punishments,' Calamitus said.

'Yes, I know,' Grogbah hissed. 'That's why I'm taking you all as slaves. Form an orderly queue!'

'You brain-bungled boggit!' Tempestra pointed her sword at the prince. 'YOU LOST!'

'Has she gone mad?' Grogbah laughed.

'It's true,' said Gladys Potts.

'We beat your guards,' Reginald Blink grinned.

'I might have a few for breakfast in the morning,' Granny said with a crooked smirk.

'Oh, yes!' Madam McCreedie said, patting her stomach greedily. 'Delicious.'

'Ooof SQUISH!' said Ooof.

Prince Grogbah's face flinched for the tiniest of

seconds. The corner of his eye twitched and he started opening and closing his mouth at a rapid pace. I could almost see the cogs whirring inside his tiny brain.

'L ... L ... L ... LOST?'

'S'right,' Calamitus said. 'You and your army of gruntygawpers have lost. Right now, my crew are taking them onboard the *Blistered Barnacle*, where they'll be fed and armed and become salty-eyed sea-donks. The only plunkling left to deal with is YOU!'

'PLEASE DON'T KILL ME!' Grogbah wailed. **'I'M TOO BEAUTIFUL TO DIE!'**

Calamitus laughed. 'Kill you?' he said. 'We're not going to kill you.'

'You're not?' Grogbah smiled with relief.

'Nope.' Calamitus walked slowly towards the prince. 'The thief of the diamond dentures has to pay a far more gut-bunkling price for their terrible crime.'

'What price?' Grogbah's bottom lip started to tremble.

'Oh, it's terrible.' Calamitus leered and clicked his diamond teeth together.

'But it's not death?'

'No.'

'Phew! At least it's not that,' Grogbah said.

'For stealing the diamond dentures, Prince Grogbah, your sentence is to spend the rest of your miserable days as Chief of Laundry onboard my ship.'

'**WHAT!?**'

'You'll sew and wash and dry and scrub, and, after a long time at sea, my crew can get VERY SMELLY INDEED!'

'KILL ME!' Grogbah howled. '**PLEASE KILL ME!**'

'Not a chance.'

With that, Grogbah brandished his sword again and started walking slowly backwards. His eyes were the size of dinner plates and he was mumbling gibberish under his breath.

'There's nowhere to go, Grogbah,' Dad said.

The goblin prince was squelching backwards

through the flower bed, waggling the sword to and fro.

''Ere, watch my flowers,' Mr Croakum grumbled from the crowd.

'STUFF YOUR STUPID FLOWERS,' Grogbah spat at him. 'I'M PRINCE GROGBAH, AND I ALWAYS WIN!'

He backed further and further away from us, swinging his sword about, until he passed into a shadowy spot with a row of thorny-looking spikes above and below it. For a second I couldn't quite make out what I was looking at, but then I realised …

'GROGBAH!' I yelled. 'COME BACK!'

'NEVER!'

The prince was walking backwards, straight into the open mouth of a snoring, sharp-toothed …

'BORGUNZA!' Mr Croakum shouted at his sleeping wife.

'MRS VENUS!' everyone joined in, but it was too late. Prince Grogbah stepped on the back of her tongue and …

GULP!

Mrs V clamped her teeth shut, swallowed and smacked her lips sleepily.

She slowly raised her enormous head on her stalk-neck and shook her tendrils awake.

'*BLEEUUGH!* I've got a horrible taste in my mouth,' she said, yawning. That's when she noticed the gaggle of guests and staff all standing below her, staring up in shock and surprise. 'Oooh, I must have nodded off. Has the prince arrived yet?'

WEIRD IS THE NEW NORMAL

Now, come on, admit it. You started this book, thinking, *WHAT A LOAD OF OLD CODSWALLOP*, and now I bet you'd love to come to stay in The Nothing To See Here Hotel.

No one really knew what to do after we'd watched Grogbah vanish into the thorny jaws of Mrs V, so we all plodded back to the wrecked reception hall and waited for someone to come up with an idea.

Nancy brought everyone mugs of steaming stag beetle tea and we scuffed about in the dust and rubble, looking a bit bamboozled.

It was Granny who finally broke the silence.

'Right! That's enough!' she barked. 'CLEAR OFF!'

Well, you weren't expecting her to say something

nice, were you?

'My bunions need their bed and I'm sick of looking at all your pukish faces ...'

'Right you are, Mrs Glump,' Calamitus said, with a grin. 'This old skrunt is ready to smell the salty sewer air again anyway.'

He shouted orders to his crew, and in no time the Squall Goblins were boarding their ship and conjuring up another magical wave to wash them back down to the water's edge.

I couldn't help but feel sad that the hero of my favourite books was leaving before I'd had time to get to know him. I watched as he clacked across the dusty tiles towards the *Blistered Barnacle*.

Captain Plank took hold of a rope hanging down from the deck above and, just when I thought he was about to climb up and leave, he turned his hollow skeleton eyes on me.

'Abraham would've been splundishly proud of you, m'boy,' he said, then beckoned me with a bony finger.

I walked over to the pirate captain with my heart

pounding in my ears.

'A small reward, methinks.' Calamitus yanked a single diamond tooth out of his dentures and dropped it into my hand.

'Keep it safe,' he said and winked. Who knew skulls could do that!? 'You never know when it'll come in handy.'

With that, he swung up onto the deck, and the last thing I saw of the Squall Goblins was Tempestra and Calamitus waving from the stern of their ship.

And that was that …

Mum and Dad set to work with the enchanted mops and brooms, and the Molar Sisters made light work of repairing the walls and staircase with their wands.

Before I knew it, everyone was plodding off to bed, and it was almost as if Prince Grogbah had never visited at all.

Don't forget what I told you right back at the start. There's always some kind of MEGA DRAMA happening at **The Nothing To See Here Hotel**, so that was a pretty average day for most of us.

Storms, and messengers, and ravens, and parties, and exploding boulders, and parades, and skinny-dipping, and plagues of hermit crabs, and criminals, and diamonds, and pirates, and heroes, and skeletons, and curses, and battles, and fireballs, and the odd person getting gobbled up are all just regular stuff for the Banister family.

Here where weird is the new normal ...

Still fancy coming to stay?

THE
NOTHING
to see
HERE
HOTEL

Steven B is an award-winning children's writer, actor, voice artist and host of World Book Day's The Biggest Book Show On Earth. When not typing, twirling about on stage, or being very dramatic on screen, Steven spends his time trying to spot thistlewumps at the bottom the garden and catching dust pooks in jars. His *The Wrong Pong* series was shortlisted for the prestigious Roald Dahl Funny Prize.

www.stevenbutlerbooks.com

Steven L is an award-winning illustrator based in Brighton, not far from *The Nothing To See Here Hotel*! As well as designing all of the creatures you have just seen throughout this book, Steven also illustrates the *Shifty McGifty and Slippery Sam* series and Frank Cottrell Boyce's fiction titles. When he isn't drawing giant spiders and geriatric mermaids, Steven loves to eat ice cream on Brighton beach looking out for goblin pirate ships on the horizon.

www.stevenlenton.com